It is likely that you received this exciting novel as a FREE GIFT from a family member, friend, youth minister, teacher, campus minister, or neighbor.

To order FREE COPIES of *My Rock and Salvation*, visit **www.matermedia.org**.

Optional donations to cover the cost of shipping are deeply appreciated.

Optional donations to help print and distribute **more free copies** of *My Rock and Salvation* are **very** deeply appreciated.

Published by Mater Media
St. Louis, Missouri
www.matermedia.org

Printing History

March 2014: 5,000 copies
June 2014: 15,000 copies

Cover and Interior Design: Trese Gloriod
Editor: Eric Gaulden

Printed in the USA.

978-0-9913542-0-7

MY ROCK & SALVATION

A NOVEL BY Zip Rzeppa

MATER
MEDIA

GRATIAS

Novels are written by people. People are empowered by the Divine, and aided by the Divine working in all of us. I'm grateful to all who helped form me before and during and after this work was undertaken and completed, and for all who helped in its creation. Gratias from my heart:

To Mater Media, our dear Mother of Media. This is your apostolate!

To the Holy Spirit for working through me and so many to create this novel.

To numerous saints and souls for your intercession.

To my late mom, Millie, for bringing the Lord's love and joy and peace into my life every day.

To my late dad, Ed, for your calm, strong example and your humor.

To my late best friend, Declan Duffy, for your prayers. The Lord has done it again, Dec!

To my best longtime friend, Bill O'Reilly, for your ever-present counsel and inspiration.

To Jane Tayon for your indomitable spirit and awesome optimism.

To Deby Schlapprizzi for your perpetual encouragement and for believing in the apostolate.

To Mary Beth Rolwes for your prayers and for making things happen in Rome.

To Greg and Don and Andy. I can always count on you, men.

To Mark Halfmann for your wisdom and counsel whenever and wherever it's needed.

To the other Halfmanns who helped, Agnes, Alex, and Sam.

To my brother, Gerry, for urging "first person."

To my brother, Joe, for plowing through drafts and advising.

To Kathleen for your love and encouragement and inspiration, and for the prayers of you and your dear mom, Pat. My prayers are with you.

To Martha Kooyumjian, my loyal friend who has such a great heart.

To my brothers in Christ from the ACTS Retreats.

To Al Barton for your support and for the title.

To Tom Bowers for your encouragement right from the start.

To editor Eric Gaulden for always wanting to get it right and for working five days a week to continually make it better.

To Trese Gloriod for the great cover design and layout and for all the things you did to bring this book into existence. You are a joy to work with!

To Maggie Singleton for jumping in with your expertise, advice, and prayers.

To Cathy Gilmore for referring me to Maggie and for your belief that we can truly make a difference.

To Vince McDonough for your trained eye.

To Steve and Debbie Rupp for your great friendship and enthusiasm. You always lift me up!

To Marty and Annette Bligh, I treasure your friendship. You serve and inspire so many.

To Lee and Marlene, how can I not feel good when I'm around you?

To John Schenk for all the connections and for believing that we can touch many souls.

To Michael James Mette for inspiring Manny Morrison to write the songs.

To Emily Wilson for helping to make the female parts ring true.

To Danielle Rose, you define beauty.

To Michael, Danielle, Emily, and Matt Maher for authentically inspiring through your music.

To each and every one of the readers of the drafts for your ideas, feedback, and perserverance.

And to every other person who helped. You know who you are. You will have your reward.

The difference between making millions in a rock band and making virtually nothing is razor thin. I'm gonna tell you my story here to show you what I mean.

But before I begin, think about this. The difference between *being* a good person, and *thinking* that you're a good person, can be huge, although most people don't seem to get that. I didn't get it for a long time. But I get it now. If you hear what I have to say, maybe *you'll* get it, too. But maybe you won't. I don't know. Each person is different. And each person is free.

Seems to me, most people *think* that they're good. Actually, most people think that they're *very* good. And a lot of them are wrong.

At the same time, I know a lot of people these days who are depressed. They either feel crappy about themselves, or they think the whole world's goin' to hell. Their problem is their thinking.

Now, if you're getting the idea that I'm a philosopher or some kind of analyst, you're dead wrong. I mean, way wrong. I'm just Manny Morrison, a singer/songwriter who lives in St. Louis.

If you can forget that I'm a musician, and if you just take a quick look, what you'll see is a guy in his mid-twenties who wears blue jeans pretty much every day.

But if you look more closely, you'll see much more than that.

I've got a good heart. I've always had a good heart. It's just that for a long time, people didn't see the goodness in my heart. And that was as much my fault as it was theirs.

I'm baring my soul here in hopes that you'll get something out of this. Maybe you will, maybe you won't. But anyway, I'm getting it off my chest.

Some of the people I've met along the way are gonna help me tell the story, and I'm grateful to them. All I can say to you is, *buckle up*, because it's a wild ride.

CHAPTER

1

♩ᵖ *Still like that old time rock and roll*
That kinda music just soothes the soul. ♪ o·

"Old Time Rock and Roll"
— Bob Seger (Stranger in Town)

Capacity: 2,000. It says so right on the wall.

The St. Louis fire marshal somehow figured that's the number for The Pageant. I guess he's counting the seating in the back, and in the balcony, but how can he count all these people on the floor, crammed against the stage?

The lights go down, and from behind the curtain, I hear the squeals, the screams, the applause. These people have come to see The Dukes! My heart is pounding out of my chest. This is our biggest gig—yet.

Show time!

The huge black curtain hits the ground, and we're in action. We open with an *explosion,* a song that blasts into the heads and hearts of everyone with ears. The crowd gets it. The decibel level rockets.

There's immediate chaos on the dance floor. Well, controlled chaos. I mean, no one's got a shotgun or anything, but arms and legs and hair are flying in every direction. I soak in the energy.

Lights flash. Strobes of red and yellow and purple bathe all those gyrating bodies. I feel a rush of heat. Heat from the lights, heat from the crowd, heat from the passion of my soul.

To my right, Big Billy Wilkinson, all 6'5" and 375 pounds of him, lays down a bass line that pulsates through the crowd. Behind me, the best little drummer in the Midwest, Crash, wails on the skins. His hands move faster than the eye can see. I strum like a madman as I move the guitar toward my hip.

I step in front of the mic, lean in, and do what I was born to do—sing. I belt it out with joy and enthusiasm. Heads bob on the dance floor. When I get to the chorus, I open up my rib cage and pour out all that I've got.

Nothing has the power to *grab* a crowd like the heart-pounding beat of rock. But I want to move 'em beyond the beat. I want the lyrics to stick to their brains, the notes to flow through their bones, the *experience* to lodge in their souls.

A fire burns somewhere deep inside me. I've been working at this for a long time, and I've still got a lot more work to do.

——————— ♪ o ♭ ———————

Backstage, I'm feeling the high from another kickass show. It feels good to have *left it all* on the stage. I'm mopping up the sweat with a terrycloth towel. I sink into a folding chair. Yeah, this is a mid-sized venue, a few miles from where I live, but I can *imagine* being backstage at the Grammys, with stars and celebrities and paparazzi.

Someone hands me a cold beer. No champagne tonight, no caviar, no limo waiting to take us to an after party—but hey, maybe someday. I *know* we're getting closer.

The metal stage door swings open. In strolls a tan, fit dude who has superstar written all over his strut. What the—? This isn't *Backstage at the Grammys,* but this *is* Steve Bronson.

You got it. The wide receiver who scored so many touchdowns with the 49ers that they started calling him "Mr. Six." And since he signed that six-year, $66.6 million free agent deal last week to play with the St. Louis Rams, Steve's sure to be called Mr. Six forever.

Well, he walks right over to Big Billy, laughs, and gives him a handshake and a backslap. For a moment, I think he's gonna give him a man-hug, but you don't want to hug Billy after a show. You'd need a shower.

Anyway, I can't believe this is happening. What the hell is *Steve Bronson* doing here? This is The Pageant, not Madison Square Garden. And while we're starting to have some success, we're not exactly the Rolling Stones.

I look at Crash over in the corner. He's got no idea he's in the presence of greatness. Crash lives in his own world. Helluva drummer, helluva loner.

"Hey, man, haven't seen you since USC!" Steve says to Billy.

Oh, yeah. I almost forgot that Billy played football for a while back in college. These days, he's dragging around a lot more mush than muscle. I mean, when that bass guitar sits on top of that gut, nobody's thinkin' about the NFL.

Billy's told me he looked like the Rock of Gibraltar back in his freshman year, before he hurt his knee. He still blames the docs at USC for pumping him full of pain killers to try to get him back on the field. Where they got him was into addiction. It's been a battle for him ever since.

"Hey, Manny, get over here!" Billy bellows.

Suddenly, I'm shaking hands with the man who caught more passes than anyone else in pro football last year. And yes, he looks pretty much like the Steve Bronson everyone's seen in the TV interviews—the blond locks over his ears, the chiseled features, the electric smile.

"Loved the show, Manny. I can't say the only reason I signed with the Rams was to see you guys in person—"

Like the 66.6 mil had nothing to do with it?

"—but it's great to see the band live. My old college bud, Billy here, sent me a video out on the coast. I guess it was a few weeks ago, and, and—"

Steve coughs. I'm wondering if he has a cold. He swallows hard, like he's got something caught in his throat. He looks down, and bites his lower lip.

He raises his eyes and looks right at me. "I want to tell you, Manny, I've got a half-brother, Barry, who *loves* that video. He loves your band. He loves your *style.*" He takes a deep breath. "He told me—when I get to St. Louis, I've got to go and see The Dukes."

I'm not sure what this is all about. "I'm, uh, glad Barry likes us."

Steve shakes his head from side to side. "No, you don't understand. See, Barry—" he swallows hard again—"Barry loves music, he's always singing—but he's got this rare disease…"

Billy's shaking his head, like he knows the story.

"…it's a muscular disease, and he's lost most of the use of his arms and his fingers." Steve pauses. "So, he'll never be able to play the guitar like you, Manny. Never be able to stand in front of a mic. But when he saw your video, he said—he said, you're exactly the kind of performer he would like to be."

I see Steve trying to hold it together. I let out a low sigh. Oh, man. I'm trying to think of something to say.

"Manny, the funny thing is, Barry looks a lot like you. His hair's a little longer—it touches his shoulders—but when I saw you on stage, I couldn't keep from thinking of my little bro, and what might have been."

I look down and exhale. I can't imagine what it would be like to know music, to love music, to have talent—and to not be able to express it. I look at Steve, and more than the most-publicized free agent in St. Louis pro football history, I see an older brother—a brother who *for sure* loves his little bro. Before I can speak, Steve says, "And here's another funny thing." He shakes his head again. "Barry's always wearing a shirt just like the one you've got on."

I don't need to look down to know what shirt I'm wearing. It's my dad's old Bob Seger shirt. Seger was Dad's all-time favorite. I feel my eyes start to mist just thinking of my old man.

I clear my throat. "Uh, Steve, if Barry likes Seger, I've got a few shirts I can send him."

Steve smiles. "Hey, man—your biggest little fan in California would love that."

CHAPTER

2

 The music moves me,
it inspires my soul,
I can't keep from singing,
that old rock and roll. ♪ o·

"Can't Keep From Singing"
— The Dukes (written by Manny Morrison)

The morning after the concert, I'm feeling pretty good—
until I go to the website of the St. Louis Gazette. The
online review of our concert is there, written by Brash
Perkins, the Gazette's backup music critic. I have no idea
how he got the nickname, Brash, but I can think of a better one for him: Ass.

He's probably trying to make a name for himself.
I'll spare you all the details, but Brash rips The Dukes
in his review. Love this line: 'Although he brought the
crowd to a fever pitch, lead singer Manny Morrison is
more stage presence and loud noise than great music.'
And here's how he described the crowd: 'high schoolers
with glazed eyes, with a fair amount of non-thirsty college kids thrown in.'

What an insult to our fans! Come on! Was he expecting to see grandmas and grandpas sipping iced tea? This guy's ridiculous. We were tight, the crowd was goin' *wild*—and this guy pans us.

As you can see, making it in the music world isn't easy. If it was, everybody'd be doing it. But I know what I've got to do. I've got to forge ahead. Gotta persist.

So I head out to Kaldi's, a coffee shop that does St. Louis proud—friendly atmosphere, comfy chairs, caffeine drinks that warm my insides. And I go to work. Okay, so it doesn't look like I'm working. It looks like I'm just sitting here staring at people. Which I am. I'm trying to capture the magic of a *person* in the words to my next tune.

But today, for some reason, the words just ain't popping. Need some java. I get up to secure a large Caramel Campanna Latte. It's espresso 700 and steamed milk blended with Ghirardelli chocolate, topped with whipped cream and a generous drizzle of caramel. It's the one that always gets me going.

But I never make it to the counter. I hear this oldies song, "Do You Love Me?" by the Contours. It came out half a century ago, but I know it, and I like it, so I start singing. Loudly. And, not really paying attention, I run smack into the most beautiful girl I've ever seen.

Well, I don't exactly run *into* her—I mean, I didn't knock her over or anything—but suddenly I'm about eight inches away from these crystal clear blue eyes. If you ask me what makes my heart stop, it's—well, everything.

10

Her brown hair, her perfect shape, the scent of her warm perfume. In one second, my senses are overwhelmed. So here I am in the presence of perfection and I'm—totally embarrassed. Because I'm still singing this crazy old song—loudly.

Do you love me?

Now that I can daaa-aaaaaa-aaaaaaance?

Damn it. I stop singing. Fortunately, I cut it off before the lyrics, *"WATCH ME NOW!"* Still, I feel like a fool. But I get lucky. Miss Beautiful gives me a shot. "So—do you always sing to strangers?"

What do I say?

"I, uh, usually only sing to strangers—when I'm on stage."

Well, I can tell she's intrigued. I can also tell she doesn't recognize me. She looks down and picks at an imaginary piece of lint on her coat. She looks me right in the face—those blue eyes are *killing* me—and says, "Well, when is your next performance?"

Tough question. Think, Manny!

"It's—tomorrow morning at 8 a.m., right here!"

If you're keeping score at home, that's two good lines in a row. She gives me this little crack of a smile, but I have no idea what it means. She picks up her latte from the counter, and heads for the door.

Now, if this was just any woman, it would be easy to let her walk, but there's something *special* about this chick. So I clear my throat.

"Hey, you gonna be here?"

She pauses, looks back, but then turns away and heads to the exit. My eyes are glued to that luscious, shimmering dark hair peeping out of the back of her coat. She gets to the door, turns, and answers with one word.

"Maybe."

Maybe? What the hell does that mean? Then she flashes me this huge smile. My knees buckle—and she's gone.

What do I do? What could I do? I pull out my phone and enter "Kaldi's, tomorrow morning, 8 a.m."

Now, I could have said the "concert" is tomorrow *night*, but I didn't want to make it look like I was rushing into a heavy date, 'cause that might scare her off. I figured I'd have a better shot with 8 a.m., because maybe she'd stop in for coffee before work. I assume she works, but who knows? Anyway, she may not even show.

──────── ♪ o 𝄢 ────────

Well, Monday morning I walk into Kaldi's at 7:50 a.m. No gorgeous babe on the scene. There are a couple of guys lugging laptops into one corner and a table of women having a meeting in another. Whoa, wait a minute. Is that *Steve Bronson* over there? It's a guy wearing a ball cap and reading the sports page, so I walk over, and sure enough—

"Hey, Steve. You learn fast. Already found the best coffee shop in town."

"Manny! Hey, man, good to see you again. Some show Friday night. I'm just trying to hide behind the newspaper here. At least it's a friend who busted me."

I feel good that Steve calls me a friend. One backstage meeting hardly constitutes a lifetime relationship. "I'll be discreet, man. Didn't know All-Pro wide receivers got up this early."

"Always been an early riser. What are *you* doing here?"

"Actually, I'm here to meet this chick. Just met her yesterday by chance. She's supposed to be here at 8. Whoa—that's her." I nod toward the door.

Our eyes whip to the stunning brunette. She's followed by a drop-dead gorgeous blonde, who moves in beside her. Clearly, they came together.

I glance at Steve. "The one I met has the dark hair. Never seen the blonde."

"That's okay," says Steve. "*I* see her."

Well, the women head to a booth and sit across from each other.

"Steve, looks like I'm gonna need a little help here."

"I'm game, brother."

So Steve and I stroll over and move smoothly into the booth. Well, at least Steve moves smoothly. Man, I'd give anything to have this guy's kind of cool.

Our butts have barely hit the seats when the blonde blurts, "You're Steve Bronson, aren't you?" Steve gives her an ever-so-slight shoulder shrug and drawls, "Yeah, girl—the last time I checked."

Well, I think the blonde is about to faint. I'm relieved when she doesn't swoon. I look at the brunette, who *really is* the most beautiful woman I've ever seen. My senses are in overdrive, but I try to be cool.

I give her a smile, and open with, "So, I'm really glad you showed up." She has no idea *how* glad. "My name is Manny Morrison."

"Nice to see you again, Manny. I'm Sheila. And this is my friend, Rachel."

"So you brought back-up."

"Well, *you* brought an aircraft carrier," she says, nodding toward Steve. It's clear the ladies have seen the news conferences or viewed some of the gazillion internet stories about Steve becoming the highest-paid Ram in history.

There's a second of awkward silence, and then Rachel says, "I love your pants, Steve."

Huh?

Sheila and I both crank to the side to look at the guy's *pants*. Well, they're either fine leather or suede, I can't tell which, but they look very expensive. Ol' Steve, Mr. Cool, shrugs and starts looking around the coffee shop. If he's the coolest guy in the place, he spots the guy who's the least cool.

"Wow, look at that guy over there. Is that the 'St. Louis look?'"

Well, the guy he's looking at is wearing *overalls*. A young guy, maybe mid-twenties. He's hefty, maybe 40 pounds overweight, with a shaved head, and a healthy brown beard. Classic *weird*.

"Oh, nooo," Rachel says. "That's not what a St. Louis

man looks like. Must be from out-of-town."

Well, as we're looking at the guy, he gets up—he's probably 6'3", about 270—and picks up his large coffee and heads our way. He nods at me and the ladies, and then stares at Mr. Six.

"Wow, you're Steve Bronson, alright. My goodness!" He's almost shouting. "It's so *great* to have you in town." He raises his right hand for a high five, but Steve doesn't respond. Totally unfazed, the guy carries on, "I'm Oscar, and I'm a *big* Rams fan." He pats his ample belly. The ladies chuckle. His face lights up with joy. "Man, the Rams are gonna kick some butt now that they've got you, man. This is tremendous. So good to meet you!"

Well, as he finishes gushing, he stumbles and his large, hot coffee spills right into Steve's lap.

"Shoot! Oh, man. I am *so sorry*. Steve, sometimes I get a little clumsy, and—"

"Yow," says Steve, grabbing for a napkin. But Kaldi's only has those thin, brown paper napkins. No Sham-Wow here.

"Damn. These threads could be ruined!" When Steve stands up, it looks like Mr. Cool has wet his pants. "I've got to find a dry cleaners—quick."

Rachel pops out of the booth and says, "Got you covered. Let's move." And in an instant, she and Steve are all but flying through the exit, followed closely by Big Daddy Overalls.

"Steve, I am so, so sorry, man. If you want to send me the bill…"

Well, now that the circus has left, here I am, suddenly alone, with Miss Fantastic—uh, Sheila. Perfect! I throw her a big smile. "So, looks like we're gonna have some time to talk."

Well, my heart sinks when she says, "Got very little time. It's already 8:15, and I've got to get to work. I certainly won't have time to catch your 'concert' today."

Cute. I'd forgotten about the "concert." "Um—so where do you work?"

"The Society of St. Vincent de Paul."

"What's that?"

"The oldest charity in St. Louis. Been around since 1845. We serve the poor, the needy, and the suffering."

"Hmm. What do you do there?"

"I'm an LCSW."

"A what?"

"A Licensed Clinical Social Worker."

I'm trying to process. "A License Clinic…?"

She rolls her eyes and cuts me off. "Look, there's no time to educate you here. Got to get to work."

No, don't leave!

Well, she tilts her head, almost like she wants to see me from a different angle. "There's *something* about you," she says. "I don't know exactly what it is." She leans forward and raises an eyebrow, ever so slightly. "Maybe I'd like to get to know you a little better. Can you meet me, let's see—Saturday, at noon?

"Uh, where?"

She puts her hand to her chin. "How about where I work?

St. Vincent de Paul's headquarters. It's on Jefferson."

"Okay." I'm struggling to put words together. "Right. Um. Uh-huh." I feel my head rapidly moving up and down. "Got it. Saturday. Sounds good." Real smooth, Manny. Real smooth.

She hits me with a smile, says "Great!" and then she takes off. And for the second time in two days, I'm watching her luscious dark hair peep out of the back of her coat as she walks out the door.

Yow-za.

CHAPTER

3

 I love the way you breathe,
I love the way you move,
You're the one I need,
to find my groove o·

"My Love"
— Manny Morrison (age 19)

St. Louis is a city filled with old buildings. To say that the "Folks Who Live to Preserve Old Buildings Society," or whatever the hell they call it, is strong—well, that's an understatement. If it's made of brick and it's still standing, well, you're gonna need a band of lawyers and a lot of dough to get a building knocked down, and even then, the odds are against you.

I'm telling you this because that's how we got our place for band practice. I'm remembering this as I strum my favorite guitar and pace around in this familiar, old, abandoned building, waiting for Billy and Crash to show up.

We're damn lucky to be here. The owner wanted to tear the whole four stories down, but since it's made of brick, the "Old Folks" group got a court order, declaring

18

this place an "Historic Building." Real funny, I know.

Well, the owner's son, a big fan of the band, gave *us* the keys. It's perfect. We drive our cars and vans right in through what used to be the "deliveries" entrance, unload our gear, and get to work. Been here two years now.

The building is on the outskirts of town, and if you spent a lot of time walking around the area without a weapon, you'd probably call it dangerous. But once you get inside, it feels good. The big, expansive, warehouse atmosphere. Somebody told me they used to gut catfish here, but the place doesn't have a fishy *smell*. The smell is more like old paint. If we stayed here 24/7, we'd probably die from asbestos poisoning.

One thing I like about the place is the feel of real wood under my boots. The floor here is oak, and it creaks in spots, but it's real. A lot of stages these days are made out of particle board. Hate that. And yeah, I know—I sing with my mouth, not my feet—but I just feel a whole lot better playing and gyrating on the real deal.

I strike a chord and listen to the reverb. Sure, the acoustics here suck, but we actually use that to our advantage. If we can sound halfway decent in *this* place, we know we'll sound at least 10 times as good anywhere else.

Billy and Crash arrive, and we engage in our secret, three-way, band practice, members only, handshake and bump. I could describe it more, but you'd think it's weird. Just know that whatever pumps you up for a practice session is good.

Anyway, what I really want you to know here is that

music is my best friend. And I know that probably sounds like a stupid way to put it. But it's what I'm all about.

Music is my high. For me, the joy of music starts inside and bubbles out to the world. Sometimes it makes me so happy that every cell of my body is dancing with joy. At other times, it soothes my nerves. Or, makes me sad. Or, restless. And it can definitely ignite feelings of tenderness and love. Big time. And all of this stuff is just the beginning of what it does to *me*.

As for others, music is how I share my gift with *them*. I write and play and sing to make people come alive. To jump around. To forget themselves. To dance like nobody's watching, even if someone is.

The process starts when I'm alone. Whatever emotion I'm feeling, I pick up my guitar and muse about it in a little song. I've come up with some cool tunes that way, although it doesn't *always* work out.

I once wrote a song about a girl I was dating. I recorded it onto a little disc and gave it to her. Boy, did that turn out to be a mistake. When I broke up with her, she sent the disc back in an envelope with one word scribbled on a piece of paper: "Liar."

Well, I'm not gonna bore you with the details, but I meant *every word* of that song when we were going out. Really and truly. But things can change, and they did, and, well—I really didn't appreciate her one-word parting note.

Anyway, every once in a few *years,* I'll write a song about someone I'm dating—I mean, someone who's really special—but I no longer take chances. I use some other generic girl's name in the lyrics. It's a *lot* safer that way.

Well, Billy and Crash are ready to go, and we push it hard for about three hours. It's great to see how we've grown together as musicians. A tight band is like a fine-tuned sports team. The various players anticipate each other's actions, and the sum becomes greater than the parts. Well, tonight we're totally in sync. We rock with a synergy and energy that almost knocks the grime off the old brick walls. We're cookin.'

For some reason, as we're finishing up the last song, Sheila pops into my mind. I have a feeling that someday I may be writing a song about her—and that I may even use her real name.

4

 On a Saturday night,
when the moon is bright,
I looked into your eyes, mesmerized,
It was just me and you.

"Saturday Night"
— Manny and the Maniacs (Manny Morrison, age 16)

Well, on Saturday, I head out to keep my appointment with Sheila. Since we're meeting at noon, it doesn't seem like a date—at least not a *date* date—but I'm excited to get to know her.

To be honest, I'm a little nervous. So I start thinking of all the things I *don't* want to do. Don't say something stupid. Don't say something that's funny to your friends but not to girls. And don't scratch your crotch, even if it itches.

I get to the St. Vincent de Paul headquarters about 10 minutes before noon. Kinda want to check the place out. Well, as I walk into the lobby of this huge, two-story building at Jefferson and Market, I'm stunned.

There's maybe a dozen chairs around the lobby. Three

are taken. There's a man dressed in old Army fatigues, with long hair and a longer beard, smelling like he hasn't had a shower in a month. Another guy, maybe about 40, is wearing a heavily stained orange jumpsuit. His tattered backpack is on the floor. The third person is a woman. I see a rip in the shoulder of her well-worn winter coat and another in the sleeve. I'm hardly trained to spot mental illness, but she's carrying on a running conversation with someone named Sadie, and Sadie ain't in the room.

Well, a middle-aged lady, probably the receptionist, appears behind a large glass window. She gives me a quick glance and then gestures to the orange jumpsuit guy. He grabs his backpack and approaches the glass. The lady opens a slot and gives him a brown bag, probably a lunch, and a bottled water. He mutters his thanks and heads out the door.

The woman, momentarily stopping her flow of words, follows. Same deal, except as she accepts her bag lunch and water bottle, she looks toward the ceiling and shouts, "Thanks be to God!" She turns and heads out, resuming her conversation with Sadie.

I shake my head and step to the window. I tell the receptionist my name is Manny, and that I'm here to see Sheila. She looks me up and down, then says she'll go and tell Sheila that I'm here.

So now I'm alone in the lobby with the shower-less guy. I sit a few chairs away from him. He stares at me for a while before he speaks. "What are *you* doin' here?"

I lean back in my chair. "Just came to meet somebody."

23

"Hmm. Anyone I know?"

Well, before I can answer, he stands up, raises his voice and says, "I got a weapon in my pocket."

Uh-oh. This can't be good. I'm wondering if he's an old war vet. My heartbeat quickens. I suck in a deep breath. I rise to my feet. He reaches into the pocket of his Army fatigues and pulls out—this big ol' pretzel.

I exhale.

He displays the pretzel in front of his chest, holding it at arm's length. He looks me in the eye and says, "If *anyone* messes with me—I give 'em the *pretzel!*"

Well, now I'm feeling sorry for the poor guy, but at the same time I'm trying hard to keep from cracking up. That's hilarious. *I give 'em the pretzel!*

And at that moment, Sheila comes through the inner door and sees me trying to hide a giggle. "Are we having a good time at St. Vincent de Paul?"

She doesn't wait for my answer, not that I had anything brilliant to say anyway, and she steps toward the man without a shower. She gives him a smile as if he's a long lost family member. His eyes light up.

"Alvin, it's good to see you," she says. "But I'm a little surprised. Your appointment with me is on Monday."

"I know."

"Today is Saturday."

Alvin strokes his long beard. He looks like he's trying to solve a great mystery. "Oh."

Sheila stands in front of him. "Alvin, did you get your lunch?"

"Already ate it," he says. Then he starts shaking his head. "Sheila," he says, "you're the greatest."

Sheila gives him a quick smile. "Thank you, Alvin. I'll see you on Monday. Now, let's go. It's noon, and we're closing up."

Alvin rises and makes his exit. Sheila pulls on her coat. "Hi, there," I say. I'm the master of opening remarks.

"Hey," she says, "thanks for coming. Done for the day." She smiles, then lets out a deep sigh. I don't know much about her job, but I can guess that it cannot be easy.

She steps in front of me. My heartbeat goes up. I watch her lips open as she says, "Feel like going for a walk?"

————— ♪ o ♭ —————

We head for Lafayette Park, about a 20-minute hike. I tell her the park is my favorite in town. She tells me she feels the same way. Sweet as sugar, right? I know. Queue the violins.

Along the way, I ask her how she came to work for St. Vincent de Paul, or SVDP as she calls it.

"Well, when I got my master's, I wanted to use it to help other people. And I knew that's what they do. You see, when I was a kid back in Cincinnati and my dad was out of work for a while, these volunteers from SVDP came to our house and helped *us* pay the electric bill."

"Got it. So do your parents still live in Cincinnati?"

"Yep." After a pause, she says, "I came here to go to St. Louis U., partly to get away from my dad. He's not a bad guy, but he's—well, he's hard to take sometimes. Kind of overbearing."

Well, I don't want to dive into *parent* stuff, so I swing it back to where she works. I tell her I really got an eyeful in my 10-minute visit to SVDP.

She shakes her head, laughs, and says, "You should come and stay for a *day* sometime."

We both put on our gloves as the wind picks up. During our brisk walk, I learn that she worked her way through school, that she's a sucker for chick flicks, and—oh, yeah—she tells me about her favorite kind of music. I don't tell her *this*—hey, you got to save a few surprises—but it's exactly the kind of rock that I play. This is *huge*.

As we enter the park, I say, "Did you know that thousands of people, sometimes as many as *ten thousand*, went to concerts here back in the 1870s?"

"How do you know that?"

I grin. "I know a lot about music."

We walk by a guy slumped over on a park bench. He doesn't look homeless—no beard or unkempt hair, no ill-fitting, stained clothing, no plastic bags full of possessions—but his eyes are glazed over. It looks like he's staring straight through us.

"Drugs are a terrible thing," I say. "I never touch the stuff."

Sheila seems surprised. "Never?"

I really didn't plan to tell her this—at least not right now—but for some reason I let it out. "My dad died of a cocaine overdose."

"Oh, my. Wow."

We walk for a couple of minutes before she breaks the silence. "Do you want to tell me about it?"

I let out a deep breath. "Well, I should tell you *this* about my dad. He was a world-class musician. Well, maybe not *world-class*, but he traveled thousands of miles making a pretty good living, for a lot of years, out on the road. But he couldn't resist the drugs. And one night, the stuff killed him."

I hear her suck in a breath. For a moment she says nothing. "Do you—"

I cut her off. "Sheila, I know I brought it up, but I really don't want to talk about my dad's death right now." And I sure as hell don't. My dad died on the floor of a motel room after his last show while I was thousands of miles away. Absolutely horrible material for a chat in the park.

Anyway, I stop thinking about my dad when we notice these two crazy squirrels chasing each other. We marvel as they fly from limb to limb, tree to tree, never hesitating, completely trusting—trusting that they'll always make it to the next branch.

I reach out and take her hand. She accepts it. Feels nice. Damn nice. We start walking across this little bridge and we stop in the middle.

"I love this park," she says.

I slip my hand out of hers and wrap it around her back. I look over the side of the bridge and imagine ducks swimming, flowers blooming, the leaves of the trees blowing in the wind. I imagine walking the pathways, sitting on a park bench, my lips meeting hers. I'm thinking how sweet that kiss could be. Yep, if this was summer, I could stay here forever with her. But this is March, and it's getting cold.

"You wanna walk to my place?"

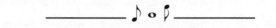

When we walk in, I see her eyes grow wide. She gazes at the wall of posters from countless concerts, the classic album covers framing the decades-old fireplace, and the rack of 14 guitars.

Her face fills with curiosity. "Are all of those guitars *yours*?"

I chuckle. "Nope, more than half of them belong to Lenny. Lenny Sanders. This is his house."

She frowns. "This isn't your house? Who's Lenny?"

"The guy that I live with here. He played bass in my dad's band ever since I was a kid. And I'll never forget what he did for me."

I lead her over to the rack of guitars. "I didn't tell you this, Sheila, but my dad's death came a week before I graduated from college. I went to Berklee, in Boston. Great music school. Anyway, my dad's old friend, Lenny, showed up at my graduation. I couldn't believe he came. Minutes after I tossed my cap, Lenny offered to let me come here and live with him. Guess he felt sorry for me."

"So, how long have you been here?"

"Three years."

She's probably wondering why I don't have my own place. I'm wondering that, too. It made sense for me to move in with Lenny when Dad died. I had nowhere else to go, and it'd take a couple of months for Dad's life insurance dough to come through. When it did, I had enough to rent a place for about a decade, but I blew 35 G's on a Camaro and bought some guitars and amps. I do still have enough to move, so, why am I still here? I guess it's because it's easy. All I have to do is pay a share of the bills.

But it isn't all great. I mean, now I got Sheila here, standing on this purple shag carpeting. It ain't as bad as bringing a date back to your parents' house, but right now—it kinda feels like it.

The only place to sit is on the red leather wrap-around couch. I take a wild guess that Sheila doesn't own one. She sits and crosses her legs.

"Would you like some coffee?"

She nods, so I brew up some fresh Highlander Grogg, and sit next to her. She's looking around the room.

"Wow, Manny, you really *are* all about music."

Oh, if she only knew.

"Music is my passion. It's like breathing for me. It's the way I express myself. Not a day goes by when a hundred different songs aren't running through my brain. I can pick up my guitar and strum all day. That's how new melodies come. That's how I write songs. But I gotta watch *people* to come up with the words. I was 'people watching' the day we met."

Sheila chuckles. "Well, you weren't watching *me,* you almost ran me over."

"Yeah, I remember." I laugh.

"So, am I going to meet Lenny today?"

"No, no, no. Lenny's only here a few days a month. Most of the time, he's on the road with his band. They're not quite as successful as my dad's band, but Lenny does pretty well."

She sits forward and takes a sip of coffee. "I know you said you didn't want to talk about it, but it had to be hard to lose your dad—right before graduation."

I appreciate the compassion in her tone. I move a little closer to her on the couch. "Sheila, I rarely talk about it to anyone, and the reason is—it's just *so hard.* My dad died in northern California. Our family home was in southern California. Lenny flew back with dad's body. Well, I'm in Boston, happily preparing for graduation, and suddenly I have to fly across the country and head to the funeral home.

"I have to stand next to Dad's casket, 'greeting' all these people, most of whom I've never met. Dad's lying there in a suit—something he never wore—and he doesn't look anything like he did during his life."

I pause for a second, thinking about how much I want to share. "Sheila, I was damn angry and confused and pissed. I just could not believe that I would never *see* my dad, or *talk* to him, or *jam* with him, ever again."

My eyes begin to fill with tears. I don't want to start crying, so I lean forward and grab my coffee. A couple of swallows help. Gotta get a grip here.

"Right after we buried my dad, I had to fly six hours back to Boston and take two finals. To this day, I have no idea how I passed. I was numb."

I slump back on the couch. Sheila's looking at me with compassion. But it's more than that. I don't use this word much, but I think I'd call it—tenderness. She puts her hand on my arm. "Manny, I can't believe how hard that must have been."

There's no way she can really know. *And so much more about my life that she doesn't know!* But this isn't the time or place to jump in about that.

By the way, here's something I should tell you. When an event or a thought or a memory touches me deep inside, I instinctively turn to music. I don't know if it's a pacifier or a distraction or a cover-up or what. I guess it's kinda like my security blanket.

So I walk over to the rack and grab my favorite acoustic guitar. I sit down on the reclining chair across from her. And I sing her a little song I wrote about my dad. Then I sing one about being a kid. Then I move over next to her on the couch, and I sing to her for about the next hour.

Now, I know you may be thinking I'm showing off, or just trying to impress her. But that isn't it at all. When I want to share, I want to sing, and that's when the guitar seems to find its way into my hands.

Anyway, I *love* the way Sheila listens, and sways, and responds to my music. I've got goose bumps as I hang up the guitar. The bumps increase when she says, "Thanks.

31

I'm glad I finally got my 'concert.'"

At this point, I'm wishing she would hang around all day and all night, but she says she's got to get ready to go to a baby shower. As suavely as I can, I tell her I'll walk her back to her car at St. Vincent de Paul.

I hope she's as happy as I am that my house is halfway between Lafayette Park and where she works. That's right. About a 10-minute walk. Miracles *do* happen.

Well, we're on the sidewalk, close to Sheila's building, when we hear the screech of brakes, followed by a woman's scream. About 50 feet in front of us, a lady is lying in the road. Another woman is bending over her. The woman straightens up and screams for help.

I react immediately, sprinting forward. As I run, I see a minivan pull over to the curb. A panicked man gets out of the driver's side and jogs toward the woman.

I get there first. The nearly hysterical woman shouts, "God, help us!" then says to me, "My mom slipped off the curb. She got hit by that van. She's not moving. Oh, please! Do something!"

I kneel over the woman. She's elderly. She probably doesn't weigh more than 100 pounds. And she's not breathing. There's no pulse.

I open her mouth like I was trained to do in CPR. I begin blowing air into her lungs. I alternate the breathing routine with a two-hand press on her chest to try to restart her heart.

On my second push, her heartbeat returns. I go back to breathing into her mouth. In no time, she's breathing on her own. I hear the wail of an ambulance siren. It seems like, within seconds, two paramedics are hovering over me.

I instantly get off my knees to let them go to work. As I rise, I see the woman's eyes open. She's feebly mouthing words that I'm unable to make out. But she's conscious!

The woman's daughter shouts, "Oh, Mom! Praise be to God!" I step up onto the curb and take a couple of very deep breaths. It is then that I realize that Sheila is holding onto my arm. She simply looks into my eyes. I'm unable to speak.

By now, a small crowd has gathered. A cop arrives and moves the bystanders onto the curb. Before long, the woman in the street is sitting up and speaking clearly.

The paramedics get a stretcher out of their EMS vehicle. The woman says she can try to stand, but the paramedics insist on lifting her onto the stretcher. As one paramedic secures her with straps, the other steps quickly toward me on the curb.

"The lady said the van only grazed her. We think she probably had a heart attack from the trauma." He turns to move the stretcher with his partner. He looks back at me, and I hear him say, "If you're the guy who got her breathing again, there's no doubt you saved her life."

I feel Sheila squeezing my arm. My head starts to nod. And then I lose it.

——————— ♪ o 𝄽 ———————

Ten minutes later, I have just about regained my composure. I'm sitting in a chair across from Sheila in her office at SVDP. She reaches out to me in a calm, soothing voice.

"First of all, Manny, what you did out there was incredible. You saved that woman's life."

I manage a weak smile. "I always thought the good ol' CPR training might come in handy someday."

Sheila scoots her chair a little closer to mine. "Manny, when you started crying, I had tears running down my face." She chuckles. "I probably would have cried more—after all, it seems like that woman's going to be alright—but I had to take care of you. I'm glad we were so near the office. It was hard to get you to stop crying."

I lean back in my chair and let out a long, deep breath. "There's a reason for that, Sheila." I feel my eyes start to water. I'm determined to hold it together. I look to the floor, then I look into her eyes. "My mom died when *she* got run over in the street."

Sheila gasps, then covers her mouth. Her eyes close. She, of course, had no idea. I mean, how could she? But she knows now.

Well, she gets out of her chair, leans over, and gives me a hug. She straightens up and looks me in the eyes.

"I'm *so sad* for you. You lost *both* of your parents." I just nod. "Manny, I can't *imagine* what that must have been like."

What can I say? "Yep. It was tough. But now you understand why, when I saw that woman, I—"

"Oh, yeah, sure. Manny, you were *heroic* to save her."

I shake my head. "I only wish I could have saved my

mom. Never had a chance." I pause. Should I tell her? "Mom was walking across a street, had the right of way, and a guy in a pickup truck ran the red light and—." I have to stop.

"No! Manny! That's so terrible. I'm so sorry. How old were you?"

"I was 14. I got to the hospital just before she died. She was on a lot of pain meds, and in and out of consciousness. But there was this moment when she opened her eyes and looked at me and said, 'Remember to love, Manny.' Those were her last words to me. 'Remember to love.'"

I see Sheila's eyes get misty. She gets up and grabs a tissue. I know this has to be hard for her to hear.

"But," I say, trying to lighten the mood, "Mom and I had a great relationship."

Sheila sits back down in her chair and sighs. "Tell me about her."

"Well, she was kind and caring. With Dad gone all the time, she pretty much had to raise me alone. We had plenty of fun together. Going to movies, shopping for toys, eating ice cream. And while it wasn't the most fun thing for me, I remember she used to take me to Mass on Sunday. And she volunteered a lot."

"Where did she volunteer?"

"Lots of places. She helped organize some races and fun runs for charity. She went on field trips with our school. She'd even drag me down to pray and give witness outside of an abortion clinic. She always did a lot of stuff at church. Some people began to think she was a religious fanatic."

"Are *you* a religious fanatic?"

I almost choke. "Uh—not exactly. I prayed to God for a miracle, that He would save Mom, and when he didn't, well, that was about the last time I ever went to church."

I see her gently shake her head. "So, after your mom died, did your dad take care of you?"

"No. He kept touring. It sucked. I had to go and live with my grandmother in Fresno. She was nice and all, but she wasn't Mom, you know? By the time I was 18, I just wanted to get the hell out of California. That's why I went to school in Boston."

I see her glance at her watch. I know she's got to go. Anyway, I don't want her to remember this as the "Dead Parents' Demise Date," and I want to leave on a happier note.

"Sheila, you're a great listener. I want you to know that I sure didn't plan to lay my parents' deaths on you today—"

She interrupts. "No, Manny, and you *probably* didn't plan on saving a woman's life, either. Or, meeting some of my homeless friends. Or, giving me a free 'concert' today. I really enjoyed that. So there's a lot of things in life we *can't* plan. But that's part of what makes life interesting, right?" Then she pauses and says, "I've really enjoyed being with you today."

I give her a smile. "I've enjoyed it, too. I would love to see you again. How about next weekend?"

"Can't. I'm going to be in Chicago." She gives me a pleasant little smile, then says, "I promised my grandmother up there that I would feed her cats while she's away."

Feed Granny's cats? In Chicago? Can't Granny's neighbors feed 'em? Does Granny live next to axe murderers?

"Well, uh, how about the following weekend?"

Now she gives me a playful smile. "Maybe."

Oh, man. Flashback to Kaldi's, our first meeting. *That 'maybe' sure turned out okay.*

I'm trying to come up with a clever response, but I don't need to.

"Manny, I'd *love* to see you then."

~ Sheila ~

Mom always said I'd probably end up with an accountant, but I always knew it would be someone more exciting. But a rock star? Well, I'm not sure Manny's a star, but after seeing his house and listening to his passion, I know he's at least a serious musician. I'm dying to hear him perform on stage.

I just love the way he looks. Smiles so easily. He could wear his hair a touch shorter, but those little curls and waves are great. And his touch made every part of me tingle!

For sure, the best thing is his eyes. I can almost see his whole life through them—the passion and the pain, the capacity for joy. He's sure been through a lot. I can't imagine what it would be like to lose both of my parents. Poor guy! But I can tell he's a survivor. Is he damaged? He sure is emotional, but he doesn't seem broken. There's a sweetness about—

Leave it to a phone call to interrupt my daydreams!

"So I can't wait to hear—rock star or phony?"

"Oh, listen, Rachel—phonies don't have 14 guitars hanging in their living room."

"Huh?"

"Oh yeah. This guy really loves his music. I guess his dad was in a rock band and toured all the time—until he died from a drug overdose. Anyway, he gave me this incredible one-hour concert after a walk in *our* favorite park! It's crazy. He's so sweet, but he's been through so much! And, of course, it doesn't hurt that he's super cute."

"Wow, this guy sounds *promising.*"

"And Rachel—I haven't told you the most incredible part. Manny saved someone's life today."

"What?"

I tell her all about Manny saving the woman in the street.

"Oh my gosh! Does this guy wear a cape? He sounds too good to be true."

"Yeah, but Dad's not going to like him."

"You can already tell? Why not?"

"Dad wants me to marry a guy in a white shirt and tie, not a guy in jeans who strums a guitar."

"Sheila, if this guy becomes a rock star, he'll be able to buy and sell that guy in the white shirt and tie."

"Right, but Dad will say, 'and if he *doesn't* become a rock star, you'll be livin' in the poor house.'"

"Sheila! You're 24 years old. Who you date and who you marry is totally up to you."

"I know, you're right. I really don't care what Dad thinks. I really like this guy."

"So are you going to see him again?"

"For sure—already set something up. That's the easy part."

"What's the hard part?"

I try to decide where to begin.

"Well, I don't want to get ahead of myself or anything, but I really like this guy, and I'm pretty sure he likes me too. At some point—probably soon—he's going to ask me to sleep with him. You weren't there when he was singing to me, Rachel. You didn't feel that chemistry. I've never felt closer to a man I just met."

"Wow. You've got it bad."

"Rachel, at some point, I may have a decision to make. It's way too soon to even *think* that someday he *may* propose marriage, but it's hard to believe I could hold him off until then. But if I try to, well, Rachel, this guy could *no doubt* move on and find somebody else in a heartbeat."

"Wait a minute, Sheila. Are you saying that you're thinking about sleeping with him?"

"Rachel, I don't know. I think, maybe—"

"Sheila! I think you better slow down, girl. You know *my* story."

"Well, I—uh, I know you lost it with a great looking guy, but there's more to my situation—"

"Oh—my—goodness! You *don't* know, Sheila. It wasn't that I just ran off and did it with some stud. He was—"

I interrupt. "The President of the Fraternity. I know, you told me."

"But *obviously,* I didn't tell you the details. He wasn't *just* the best looking guy in the world, he wasn't *just* the Frat King, he was the *first love of my life!* Sheila, you know how your guy Manny has all those guitars? Well, my guy, Kurt, had his art hung all over his walls. His own *paintings.* Beautiful stuff. Oh, he was so talented. And sure, I could imagine wedding bells.

"You know, Sheila, regarding sex, I was kind of where you are right now. But here's the difference. I was madly in love, *much* farther along than you and Manny, and I was wavering, thinking—I've never gone all the way, but with this guy, someday, some night, some time that just feels right—well, maybe I'll have sex with him. Well, one night, after I had quite a bit to drink but still knew what I was doing, we had sex.

"Now, here's what I never told you, Sheila. This great guy, this fabulous artist—who I *thought* was the love of my life—drops me a week later, picks up with some bimbo, and then lets all 90 guys in the fraternity know how he 'conquered' me.

"Do you know how horrible I felt inside? I was destroyed! And do you know how embarrassed I felt just walking to class? I felt like everyone on campus was judging me."

"Oh, Rachel. I didn't know—"

"Sheila, you've got to take your time, and think about things."

"Rachel, I'm thinking about a *lot* of things. Probably too many, too soon. I can just sense that he likes me. A lot. And I can already tell I like him. A lot. He really fascinates me. All I know is that if his band is any good—or even if it isn't—I want to be much more than just one of his groupies."

"Do you know if he even *has* groupies?"

"No, I have no idea. But he played the Pageant last week, and I'm sure he'll be playing at other places, so it'll be *awfully easy* to find out."

"Yeah, that's for sure. But back to—you know. So you're not committed to waiting until—"

"Well, I want to, but I just have a feeling that he's not going to agree, and that he may move on."

"Well, Sheila, if he won't wait, then he isn't good enough for you."

"Huh. Is any guy these days willing to wait? Look, Rachel, I wouldn't lose it to just *anybody*. It's just—this guy is different. He doesn't seem like the type to sleep with me and move on. Maybe it would be worth it."

"But don't you see, Sheila? That's exactly what I was trying to tell you earlier. I waited to have sex with a guy *I* thought was just right, too—and it was so *not* worth it."

"Oh, Rachel, I feel for you. And I appreciate you sharing. I'm blessed to have you as a friend. I don't know. As for Manny, there's no way to predict the future. All I can tell you is, I'm super into him, and I just have a feeling this isn't going to be a short-term deal."

CHAPTER

6

 Fast cars, lots of girls, fine cigars,
diamonds and pearls,
On top of the world, ya gotta know,
I'm here to stay, you can't say no.

"Here to Stay"
— The Dukes (Manny Morrison)

Two seconds after I wake up on Sunday morning, I'm wishing Sheila was next to me. She's smart, confident, caring, and certainly beautiful. The most interesting thing is—well, I can't really explain it. Some might call it the "it" factor. And she's certainly got "it." And I can't help myself. I want "it."

Anyway, Steve Bronson is coming to pick me up for brunch. He's probably expecting something upscale, so I'm gonna take him to the Ritz Carlton. *Puttin' on the Ritz.*

Well, my eyes pop when Steve picks me up in his black Lamborghini. Damn. And I was thinkin' my Camaro was nice.

The doors open like a spaceship. The interior reminds me of a cockpit. I recline in the orange leather seat. Ev-

43

erything is either leather or suede—the console, the door panels, the steering wheel.

"Never been in a machine like this, Steve. How much do these things cost?"

"This is the Aventador model. Top of the line." He looks at me and raises his eyebrows. "Less than half a million."

"Oh, good."

Steve revs the engine, and we achieve "takeoff." We wheel onto the highway and shift into "Purr." Man, what a ride!

I look over to the superstar. "Hey, California Man, I sent your little brother some Seger shirts."

Steve smiles warmly as he adjusts his designer sunglasses. "Oh, great. Thanks. I know Barry'll like 'em."

Well, I'm pretty sure the kid will. One was a Seger special from his early days. Another was from his gigantic tour in 1983, with all 76 tour stops written on the back. The third one was—well, I get emotional over this one. It's from a festival Seger headlined. My dad was the opening act. I thought long and hard about keeping the shirt, but then I remembered how Dad would toss guitar picks and stuff to the fans in the handicapped section when he played. So I thought—in the name of my dad—I'd "toss" this shirt to Barry.

With the touch of a finger, Steve changes the music selection from rock to light classical, and shoots me a look. "So, how did it go yesterday with the brunette?"

I tell him that Sheila was great, that I visited her office, and that we walked through the park. I left out the parts about saving the woman and crying about my mom. Hey, you don't have to tell everyone everything.

Steve smiles. "You gonna sleep with her soon?"

Well, I'm a little taken aback by his question. I mean, I understand that Steve Bronson is fast—fast on the field, fast in his car, and it looks like *very* fast with women. But I'm not Steve. And *I'm* the one who's going out with Sheila. So I just say, "We're going out again in a couple of weeks."

Steve drops the subject. We arrive at the entrance to the Ritz, and he coolly hands the parking valet $50. Guess that's enough to protect the hubcaps.

Well, we walk into the hotel lobby, and Steve causes a mob scene. All these women *migrate* to him. I know, he's got wealth and muscles and sexy blond hair, a west coast tan, and he just *looks* like he can run faster than a cheetah. I get it. And I must be invisible.

Actually, I'm amused as the women put their arms around Steve and insist that their husbands and boy-friends take pictures. What's really funny is that the guys are even *more* excited when they get *their* pictures taken with him. Hey, it's been a long time since the days of Kurt Warner in St. Louis, and everyone's expecting Mr. Six to get the Rams back to the Super Bowl.

We seek refuge in the Ritz restaurant. As we enter, we're ambushed by a female newspaper reporter. A nice looking female reporter. "Steve, I'm Cindy Harris, St. Louis Gazette, and I—"

"Look, I just came here to eat brunch," Steve tells her.

Well, she all but bats her eyes and says, "I just need 10 minutes. Everybody's writing about you, but I want to do a story with a little different slant. I want to do a story about you and your brother."

His brother? *Barry?* The one who's getting my Seger shirts?

Steve raises an eyebrow and says, "Okay, I'll give you 10 minutes. Manny, hope you don't mind. Let's go find a place to sit."

The host leads us to a table for four by the floor-to-ceiling windows. Cindy the reporter is young, maybe 25. Her blonde hair barely touches her shoulders. She's wearing a long black skirt with a purple blouse buttoned nearly to the neck.

A waiter comes by and begins to describe the sections of the buffet spread, but Steve cuts him off. "I'm just going to have coffee for now. Anyone else?" The reporter and I both nod. Cindy's gonna get her interview, but not brunch.

"Steve, I'm grateful that you're doing this. I won't waste your time. A reporter out on the coast told me you and your brother both have the same disease. Is that right?"

Same disease?

Steve takes a drink of water. "That's right. But my brother's case is far more severe."

Cindy knocks some words into her tablet. "What kind of disease is it?"

"It's a rare muscular disease. I can't even spell it. It's genetic, from my mother's side. It impairs motor functions. My brother can walk, but not too fast, and he tires easily. He's got weakness in both arms, so he has limited dexterity there. I was telling Manny here about his great love of music, but he'll never be able to play a guitar."

She nods. "That's really sad. So, Steve, the disease was not related to your dad at all?"

I see a slight wince on Steve's face at the mention of his father. "No."

"Your father was Brady Dillon."

Steve snorts. "Yeah, if can call him a *father.* He knocked up my mother—and I'm only telling you this because I know you'd find out anyway—and then he took off. You've got seven minutes left. What else?"

The reporter looks him right in the eyes. "Look, Steve, I just report the facts. Brady Dillon played 10 years in the NFL. That's a fact. But don't worry, this is not a story about derelict dads, no matter how famous they are. What I want to know is, how you overcame this disease."

The waiter serves the coffee. Steve studies the reporter's face for a moment, then gives her a slight smile. "Okay. I'll tell you about that."

He pours some cream, leans forward, and lowers his voice. "When I was two-years-old, I had braces on both legs, and the docs said that I might have to wear them for the rest of my life. But my mom was so loving, she was determined that I'd be just like all the other kids. So she found this great therapist, and he'd walk me up and down the beach every day. Before long, he took the braces off, and made me walk on my own."

I lean back in my chair. Wow, I had no idea. I can't imagine.

Steve continues, "The doctors were amazed at my progress, but the therapist didn't stop there. When I was five, I was *running* in the sand by the ocean every day. And I just never stopped. By the time I was a senior in high school, I could run faster than any kid in the state."

The reporter is nodding. "But you've got to have more than speed to play at USC."

I can tell this Cindy knows her stuff. Steve smiles. "That's right. The fact is, USC didn't offer me a scholarship, but that's where I wanted to go, so I walked on. My mom cried tears of joy when I made the team, but that wasn't enough for me. Freshman year, I was fourth-string behind three McDonald's high school All-Americans, so I red-shirted. And then I took my beach training to the extreme."

Cindy is typing furiously into her tablet. "What did 'extreme' look like?"

Steve runs a hand through his thick hair. "Well, I'd run in the sand, which is hard enough, but I did it wearing weights around my ankles. Then, I'd head to the mountains, and I'd run up and up and up until I'd puke." He gives her a wink. "You can call it 'vomit' if you'd like." Cindy smiles.

"Then, I'd head back to my high school where my old coach would let me catch balls shot out of the supersonic pass-catching machine. In high school, I'd stand about 12 yards away. But now I moved up to eight yards. Almost unheard of. And I practiced so much, I began catching the ball with one hand. First the right hand, then the left. So, when I got back to USC, making those incredible catches seemed almost easy to me."

Cindy finishes typing and looks up, her hands still on the keys. "So the disease never flared up?"

"Nope, never. I'm a lot luckier than my little brother."

Cindy asks him a couple of other questions about his college career and the draft, then wraps it up. When she's out of earshot, Steve says, "Sorry about that, Manny. In a couple of years, when you're famous, you'll find reporters sitting in restaurants just waiting for *you* to show up."

I can only dream.

The restaurant GM hurries over. "Welcome to the Restaurant at the Ritz, gentlemen." He's beaming. "Mr. Bronson, if you'd like, I can keep all other reporters away. And I can have my staff bring you brunch if you don't want to battle the buffet line."

Steve thanks him, but says, "Nah. I've run over plenty of defensive backs. I think we can survive the food trough."

I look at Steve and shake my head. "Man, you live some kind of life."

Steve sighs and chuckles. "Yeah, it's crazy, alright."

"I've never heard that story before. You poured out a lot of sweat, man."

"Well, *you* know something about sweat. You were working pretty hard last week at the Pageant."

I nod. "Well, yeah, but it's a different kind of work. I mean, when we're on stage, I don't have linebackers trying to knock the pick out of my hand, but I definitely need a shower after we're done."

Well, we go and fill up our plates at the buffet line. We make it back to the table without anyone trying to tackle Steve.

When we sit down, Steve's jaw drops. "Oh, no."

"What?"

"Nine o'clock and headed this way."

I look up and I can't believe it—it's the guy in the overalls who doused Steve with coffee at Kaldi's.

"It's Oscar."

I can't believe Steve remembers his name. Well, we both go speechless as Oscar saunters over with a plate stacked with an absurd amount of food.

"Steve, man, how you doing? And, good to see you again, uh…"

"Manny."

"Hey, you guys don't mind if I join you, do you?"

Well, I guess we're just too shocked to speak before he plops himself in a chair.

Steve recovers and starts chiding him. "Didn't know they let folks in here wearing overalls."

Well, Oscar smiles. I mean, he's being insulted and he's still looking as happy as if he'd just won the lottery. He gets this crap-eating grin on his face, and leans forward like he's gonna say something really important. "Man, I get in *everywher*e in my 'ralls. Yep, sure enough do." He's shaking his head like he's amazed he gets in anywhere. "Boy, this buffet is fantastic, huh?"

You know, this guy's pretty weird, but somehow he's hard to hate. Steve lets out a little laugh and says, "You got that right, Oscar. This buffet can stand up to anything I saw out on the coast."

Our plates are so full I'm having trouble deciding where to start.

"Guys?" We look at Oscar. "Guys, guys, guys—do you mind if I pray before we dig in?"

I suck in a deep breath as Steve and I look at each other, and we both slowly put down our forks. We watch as Oscar bows his head. "Father, I just want to thank you for my friendships with Steve and Manny." Just for fun, I kick Steve's foot under the table. "Father, I ask you to bless Steve and the Rams in the upcoming season. And Father, I want to ask you to bless this food."

I'm thinking, okay, that was nice, and I'm about to pick up my fork when Oscar continues. He's looking at his plate as he says, "Father, I just want to thank you for *all* of this food you are blessing us with. I want to thank you for making the chicken that produced these eggs." Steve and I raise our eyebrows. "And Father, I want to thank you for making the pig from which this bacon and these delicious sausage patties came." I give Steve the stink eye. This is weird. "Thanks for the cow you made just for us, to provide us with this great beef." Oh, boy. "And for the orange trees from which came the orang-es whose juice was squeezed into our glasses." I start to clear my throat. "And, Father," Oscar lowers his voice a bit, "I want to thank you for the men and women who went out and picked those oranges, and brought them in from the field." Oh, brother. "And for the guy who drove the oranges to the airport." Is he kidding? "And for the pilot who flew the oranges to St. Louis." Come on. "And for the guy who got them off the plane—and for the guy who drove them to this restaurant—and for the guy who squeezed these oranges this morning—Father, this orange juice is *fresh*-squeezed!" I'm rolling my eyes. "And finally, Father, we thank you for all the chefs and servers who have cooked this feast and brought it to the buffet table for us to enjoy." Oscar raises his eyes and bellows, "Amen!"

I slap my forehead. Steve gets this wry grin on his face and says, "Oscar, you forgot the guys who grew the coffee beans, and brought 'em in, and—"

Oscar gives a clap of his huge hands. He smiles and says, "Thank you, Steve, you're right! 'Oh, Father, thank you for the beans, and the ground they grew in, and the growers and the grinders, and for all those who got us this coffee.'" Then he looks at me, and he looks at Steve, and he leans forward and says, "You know, guys, it took *a whole lot of folks* to get us this brunch this morning."

Well, Steve gives me a look that has "this is the craziest stuff I've ever heard" written all over it. But I don't know. Maybe Mr. Overalls has a point.

Anyway, we chow down on the food. While we eat, only three people come over to ask Mr. Six for his autograph. Me and Steve decide to check out the exotic dessert buffet while Oscar finishes up the mountain of food on his plate.

We start to graze at the dessert bar. Cakes, pies, mousse, ice cream, French pastries, anything you can imagine. I grab some pineapple-upside-down cake and a piece of pecan pie. Even though it's the off-season, Steve exhibits amazing discipline in selecting the biggest bowl of low-fat, low-cal frozen yogurt I've ever seen, and we head back to rejoin Oscar.

When we get to the table, he's gone. We're thinking, he's probably back in the buffet line. He'll be the easiest guy in the place to spot. But we don't see him. Oh, well.

As the waiter comes over, Steve says, "Manny, love this place. Let me pick up the check."

"No need for that, sir," says the waiter. "The gentleman in the overalls already took care of it."

Steve winks. "I think my opinion of Oscar is improving."

We're getting up to leave and Steve says, "Hey, you're leaving a piece of pineapple there."

"Yeah, so?"

Steve grins. "Do you know how many guys it took to get that pineapple to your plate?"

CHAPTER

7

♩· ♭ *My phone is ringin', They wanna know,*
Are the big boys ready? It's time to go. ♪ 𝅝·

"Big Boys"
— The Dukes (Manny Morrison)

I'm not happy that I have to wait two *weeks* for date number two with Sheila. Feeding felines in Chicago? She *sure* must love her Granny.

Anyway, I pour my passion into my music. I'm home, strummin' away on my favorite guitar, trying to work out the kinks in a new song.

My phone vibrates. It's Sonny Jenkins, my agent. The one who we're counting on to make us famous. He's not doing a very good job. We've been with him for two-and-a-half years now. I really don't trust the guy, but he works cheap. I often think about getting rid of him, but good agents are hard to find.

I can hardly hear Jenkins over the din of wherever he is. No doubt, some low-life bar. I crank up the volume on my phone to full.

"Manny, big boy, got a great gig for you! This Saturday! Chicago! That's right, Chi-town. I got you into the March Rock Fest at the United Center. You're opening the show!"

I frown. Now, I know you think I should be doing cartwheels or something, but I know my agent. Nothing is ever as good as he paints it.

"Okay, Jenkins. So—what's the catch?"

"The *what?* The catch? I can't believe you, Manny. I'm making you big. I'm getting you in front of the whole world here! This is a big deal."

"Okay. But what exactly *is* the deal?"

"The deal's great. All expenses paid. Flight. Hotel room. The works. Huge crowd! Thousands!"

"Jenkins, how much are they paying us for this?"

"Well, it's an expensive flight. Last minute. And the hotel room is great, Manny. You're gonna love it! Top of the line!"

"Jenkins, how much?"

"Well, after all that, and after my *small* fee, you're technically playing the show for free."

"For *free?* As in *zero?* You're saying *nothing?*"

"Manny! Think of the exposure!"

I hear glass breaking in the background and someone screaming Jenkins' name.

"Listen, Manny, uh, I gotta go. Got another client on the other line."

And then he just hangs up!

My head is swimming. Chicago. The Rock Fest. *Great.* First band on stage. Yeah, but that's bad. There'll be about 15 bands playing that day, and nobody remembers the opening act. Still, there will be thousands there, even for the first band. Exposure, hell yes. But—no pay? He's gotta be kidding. But I know Jenkins. He ain't kidding. I wonder what his *small fee* is anyway. But wait a minute—did he say Saturday? Holy shit! Sheila's gonna be up there! Wow, she can come to the Fest. She can see that I'm for real!

I put my trusty guitar back in the case and plop down on the couch. The band's gonna be excited. Not about playing for free, that's for sure. But still, it'll be great exposure for us.

Let's see, what songs are we gonna go with? How long's the set? Damn that Jenkins, as usual, he leaves out the details. Well, I guess we're gonna find out if my songs are good enough for the masses. That's a little scary. What if they're not? Hey, they sound *great* when we're practicing—but we don't practice at the United Center.

Breathe, Manny.

———— ♪ o ♭ ————

"Sheila, it's your favorite rock star."

I can tell she was not exactly expecting me to call at 10:30 on a Sunday night.

"Oh, hi, Manny. What's up?"

"Just wanted to say, I'm really looking forward to seeing you this Saturday."

"Manny, you mean, *next* Saturday."

"No, I mean *this* Saturday."

"I told you I'm going to be in Chicago this weekend."

"Yeah—so am I." I love surprises.

For a second, she says nothing. "Oh, Manny, you can't *do* that. I don't want you to go all the way to Chicago just to see me."

I laugh. "Well, I'm not going *just* to see you. I'm coming to rock Chicago."

"Manny, what are you talking about?"

I pause here for dramatic effect. "Sheila, me and the band are opening the March Rock Fest at the United Center."

I hear her gasp. "Manny! You didn't tell me you were going to—"

"I just found out tonight. Haven't even told the band. You're the first person I called."

There's a pause, then a little laugh. "Manny, I don't know what to say. Wow. Just—wow!"

I wish she could see my smile. "I'd love for you to come and see us. I'll get you a pass. It's gonna be great!"

"Manny, this is wild. Of course I'll be there!"

"Great. Listen, Sheila, I'd love to talk, but I've gotta call the band. This is something they should probably know about."

She laughs. "Ya think?"

CHAPTER

8

 Big city, big city, I can see you shine,
Pretty girl, pretty girl,
wanna make you mine.

"Pretty Girl"
— The Dukes (Manny Morrison)

This is my first trip to Chicago. It's got 9,729,825 people. I know, I Googled it. But Chicago is much more than a whole bunch of folks. It's got character. I mean, where else would people flock to see a baseball team that hasn't won the World Series since 1908? And you know how a lot of places serve green beer on St. Patrick's Day? Well, here they dye the Chicago *River* green. They've got an organized tour of chocolate shops (more Google research), and they hold this widespread belief that deep dish Chicago pizza is the greatest pleasure on earth. May have to check that one out.

I get jazzed just *thinking* about the Chicago music scene. The three-day summer Blues Festival by the lake is legendary. And I'd love to go see a couple of pals of mine from Berklee who landed spots in the Chicago

Symphony. And what I'd really like to do—and I know you're gonna say I'm dreaming—is to play outdoors at that Pritzker Pavilion.

I have no idea who the hell Pritzker is, but he built a helluva pavilion. Revolutionary. Like 4,000 seats, room for 7,000 more on the lawn, with a truly one-of-a-kind sound system. The speakers are strung overhead, so that the lovers on the lawn can hear the sound just as clearly as the big-wigs in the front row. Boy, I'd love to hear the tunes of The Dukes pouring out of that. But only the cream of the crop, the best of the best, get to play there, and that's not us—not yet. But damn, we gotta be getting closer.

We fly in the day before our gig. I discover Jenkins' definition of a "top of the line" hotel. Plaster is peeling off of the walls. "No smoking" signs are everywhere. I'm guessing about 10 million guests couldn't read. And somebody must have lost the phone number for the car-pet cleaning service about a decade ago.

But who cares where we sleep? We're up here to play, and that's what we're going to do. Me, Billy, and Crash head to the United Center to see the venue. Jenkins meets us at the performers' door. We walk into the arena and stare at 20,000 empty seats. Tomorrow, this place will be too loud to hear yourself think. But right now, it's about the quietest place I've ever been in.

I hear the echo of my boots as I walk across the stage. I envision the lights, the crowd, women screaming my name. It's what I've been working to get to for *so* long.

The adrenaline is already flowing.

I look to my bandmates. Big Billy is gazing at all those empty seats, and he looks like he's gonna puke. Crash's eyes appear to be in a catatonic state. Damn! They're scared shitless. Not good. Gotta try to inspire a little confidence here.

"We're gonna kill it tomorrow, guys." They respond with hesitant smiles.

Then *I* start to worry. What if we bomb? What if the sound system fails? What if they're just using us as a *sound check?* Are these songs as good as I think they are? Am *I* as good as I *think* I am? Will Sheila want to date me if I fail?

Man, there's a lot riding on this. Twenty years of playing the guitar, not to mention the most beautiful woman I've ever known, could go right down the tubes in 20 minutes tomorrow.

But hey, I can't let Billy and Crash know that I'm nervous. I'm the leader of the band. Gotta pump 'em up. "Listen, guys—who knows where tomorrow's gonna launch us!" I clap my hands with enthusiasm. The sound echoes through the empty arena. "Hey, no worries, guys. Seriously. We got this." I nod my head with vigor and certainty, as if I had just said, 'My name is Manny.' "Loosen up, boys. Go out and enjoy the city. I'll see you back at the hotel tonight and we'll go over the set list."

Whew. Glad that's over. You know, I rarely get nervous. But boy, we got some pressure goin' on here. I gotta get some food.

I'd made plans to meet Sheila at this restaurant, Petterino's, at one o'clock. I know nothing about the place, but Sheila says it's damn cool. She's probably had lunch there with Granny. I'm amused by the sign in the window.

'Open till 3 a.m. Sympathetic bartenders.'

I head inside and Sheila's waiting for me. Man, she looks fabulous. And she's right about Petterino's. The place has class. A large, ornate bar with every stool occupied. Tables with window views of the busy sidewalks. The walls are filled with framed caricatures of famous people. I fantasize that maybe someday my mug will be hanging up there. But—not if I blow it tomorrow.

While we eat, I confide my fears to Sheila. I see the concern in her face. She says, "I know what we should do. After lunch, I wanna take you somewhere."

So after lunch we walk down State Street, take a right on Madison, and go about five blocks. She stops suddenly and says, "Look up."

I stop dead. My eyes move to the largest crucifix I've ever seen in my life. The cross starts about 15 feet off the ground and extends about 30 feet up from there. It must be about 20 feet wide. It looks like the image of Christ is made of marble and set into a limestone facade.

"Sheila, what is this place?"

"St. Peter's in the Loop. A good old Catholic church."

I've never seen a church wedged between two skyscrapers.

"Are you Catholic?"

She gives me a big smile and says, "Yep!"

61

"Sheila, what are we doing here? This isn't Sunday."

"It doesn't have to be Sunday to pray."

What is she talking about? "Why do you think we need to pray?"

"You're nervous, aren't you?"

"Well, yeah. What does that have to do with praying?"

"Manny, you've got great talent, but that talent comes from God." Oh, man. She sounds like my mom. "Believe it or not, God can help you tomorrow, but," she smiles, "there's a better chance that'll happen if you ask Him."

Is she kidding? "Sheila, I don't know. The last time I prayed was when my mom got killed—and it didn't work."

She lets out a quick breath. "Manny, I can't explain to you why bad things happen to good people, but I know this: there is a God, and He can help you."

I'm not so sure. Anyway, I haven't been in a church in 11 years, but I know I'm going to be in this one because Sheila steps up and opens this huge door and nods to me as she holds it open.

I hear the door creak as it closes behind us. Right away, I know this place has been here for years. Lots of years. It's got kind of a musty smell. The walls and floor and ceiling had to be constructed decades ago.

We're standing in the hallway or whatever they call it, right by the inner doors.

"Manny, you told me your mom was Catholic. She took you to church, right? So—I assume you received Holy Communion?"

Where is she going with this? "Well, yeah, sure. I even remember my First Communion. All of us little boys had to wear blue suits and all of the girls, white dresses."

"I bet you looked precious."

Haven't thought about *that* lately. "Maybe I did. Um, I don't know, it was such a long time ago."

She wraps her arm around my elbow. "So, Manny, do you believe that our Lord is truly present—body, blood, soul, and divinity—in the Blessed Sacrament?"

Wow, this is deep! I'm trying to think. Yeah, the words sound vaguely familiar. I haven't thought about Catholic stuff in years. I'm trying to remember, and I want to be straight with her, and some of it starts coming back.

"Um, Sheila, I probably believed that the host was Jesus' body back when I was little. I remember Mom teaching me that. But that doesn't change the fact that God didn't spare my mom, and I haven't even been *in* a church since she died."

I see her big, stunningly beautiful eyes fill with compassion. Gosh, she doesn't need to speak. But I watch her lips part, and our eyes lock, and she says, "Manny— please hear this: When we go into the church, you will see me kneel in front of the host. It looks like a white wafer, and it will be displayed in a container made of gold. Manny, I truly believe that Jesus Christ turned that little piece of unleavened bread into His body in a great, great miracle that only God could do, so that He could remain with us after He ascended into heaven."

Her voice sounds nothing short of angelic, and the

words sound so sweet. And yet, it doesn't make sense. "How could Jesus turn that piece of bread into His body when He left the earth 2,000 years ago?"

I see her smile gently as she looks into my eyes. "Manny, He does it through the priest, who takes the place of Christ during the Mass. Remember when you went to Mass with your mom—"

"Yeah. Sort of. I mean, I went and all, but I can't recall a whole lot."

"Manny, I can tell I'm taxing your brain. For now, let's just go inside. You can kneel before Jesus or just sit and pray while I kneel. I want to ask God to help you tomorrow."

I feel my head shaking left to right, but there's no way I can say no.

Well, we go in, and it's just like she said it would be. She walks to the front of the church and kneels. I sit and stare at the host in the gold thing. I glance at Sheila. I'm not sure I know what praying looks like, but I'm guessing it looks *exactly* like what she's doing right now. I just sit there and watch. Before long, I relax and start to look around. After a few minutes, I look at the host and say— silently of course—"Jesus, I don't know if that's you or not, but if it is—help us to play well tomorrow."

Well, the exact second I say that in my head, I see Sheila make the sign of the cross. She turns, smiles at me, and stands up to leave. I feel a little dazed as we walk out of the church in silence. I can't help but notice that we're passing a couple of dozen people of all ages and races, kneeling or sitting, staring at that wafer.

Now I get why they call this the Windy City. I'm glad it's March and not January, but I'm still freezing here. Don't want the golden throat to get sore. Then Sheila hits me with another surprise.

"Manny—you want to get high?"

"Um, uh—what?"

She gets this gleam in her eye and says, "Follow me."

We walk for a few blocks and I'm worrying about my vocal chords turning into icicles. Finally, we stop and she says, "Look up."

I wonder if I'm about to see another giant crucifix. Instead, it's a giant building. Huge. She drags me inside. We're in the Willis Tower. She says it's the second tallest building in the country, and we're heading up. Fortunately, we take an elevator.

We get to the observation deck on the 103rd floor, and my jaw drops. Floor-to-ceiling glass walls on every side. Down below, the people look like ants, and the cars look like—slightly bigger ants. Lake Michigan stretches farther than we can see. From here, the other skyscrapers remind me of little kids looking up at their parents.

Sheila pulls me into a short line, and I'm wondering what we're waiting for. Well, in a couple of minutes, we step out onto what they call "The Ledge." It's this all-glass balcony. There's nothing below us except a sheet of Plexiglas. Sheila says we're 1,300 feet above the street. I'm just hoping the guy who installed the Plexiglas wasn't drinking.

Once I'm confident we're not going to end up as splats on the sidewalk, I take a deep breath. I look at Sheila. I can't believe how her hair shimmers. There's this light in her eyes. She looks *beyond* beautiful! *Way* beyond. I look to her lips and I just want to kiss her.

But just at that second, two old, fat guys move in to share the balcony. Damn. Kinda kills the mood.

We take the supersonic elevator to the ground. When we get back outside, the sun is starting to dip below the skyscrapers. In my heart, I want to spend the rest of the day and night with her, but the biggest gig of my life is about 18 hours away.

"Sheila, this has all been great. I hate to say it, but I've got to get back to the hotel."

She teases me. "Right now?"

Man, I'd really like to say, well, no, let's run around town, and go to dinner, and—but I can't. "Sheila, I'm the singer and the lead guitarist and normally I'd be rehearsing long and hard for a gig like this, but I haven't had time. I've got a lot to go over tonight."

Suddenly, her luscious lips shoot forward and meet mine. But just for an instant. "I understand. So, what's up for tomorrow?"

I'm thinking about that kiss. "Um, can you meet us at the hotel at 8 a.m.? You can't be late, 'cause things will be moving fast."

"Got it." Her big smile kills me. "See you then, Mr. Rock Star."

CHAPTER

9

 We're gonna rock it, rock it,
rock it on through,
When I see you dance,
I wanna do da dance, too
When I see you dance,
I wanna dance with you.

"Rock It Through"
— The Dukes (Manny Morrison)

The next morning, I hear a crash and I cringe. Billy has been following me through the hotel lobby toward the door. I turn around to find his 375 pounds spread-eagled on the floor. Must have slipped on something in our "top of the line" hotel. The amp we need for our performance is lying next to him. I make sure the amp is okay, and then I go to help my favorite whale. As I'm down on my knees trying to assist Billy, crane style, Sheila walks into the lobby. Right. Timing is everything.

"Uh—hi. Sheila, I'd like you to meet Billy."

"I can see you two have a close relationship."

When we're back on our feet, I make a more formal

introduction. "Sheila, Billy's the best bass player in the Midwest. You'll see today."

"Can't wait. Where's the rest of the band?"

"We only got one other guy, our drummer. You'll meet him soon. Gotta warn you. He's the silent type. His name is Crash."

She raises her eyebrows. "Crash? Crash what?"

"Just Crash. The guy just crushes the skins."

She puts a finger to her chin. "Then why don't you call him "Crush?""

Good question. Before I can come up with an answer, Crash, all 140 pounds of him, slinks out of the elevator and wanders toward us.

The ever-friendly Sheila breaks into a smile. "Hi, Crash!"

"Hey." And he walks right past us.

"I see what you mean, Manny."

The band's all here, but now the guy we're waiting on is Jenkins. He's got our passes. Without him, the opening act is going to be an empty stage. We're supposed to be out of here, and where is he? He should be worrying about us, *his band*, and we're worrying about *him*.

I call his room. No answer. Shit! Does he know what day this is? I've got enough to worry about without—

"Manny—there he is." Billy's voice is filled with disgust.

I look across the lobby. Jenkins is chatting up a perky desk attendant who is *obviously* doing her best to ignore him.

"Jenkins!" Damn. Here I am straining my vocal cords.

"Jenkins, what are you doing?"

Sheila's eyes widen. "That's your agent?"

"Well, at least for now." Jenkins is eyeing Sheila as he approaches. He has enough oil in his hair to lubricate a Chevy. Just love how his middle-age paunch extends over the Sansabelt slacks. He probably thinks the plaid jacket is hot.

"We gotta get outta here. Sheila, this is Sonny Jenkins."

Jenkins slyly looks at her chest as they shake hands. I feel like punching him, but I don't have time.

"Jenkins, do you have the passes?"

"Of course, superstar. You know I always take care of you."

Yeah, *sure.* I don't have time for this right now.

"Let's go."

_____ ♪ o ♭ _____

When *you* go to a concert, you go to have a good time. When *I* go to a concert, I go to work. This is my job, and my job is to make you dance. To do that, I've got to have my guitar sounding tight.

So it's half an hour before we go on, and I'm on this huge stage way up off the floor, tuning up. I plug in to the sound system, and I strike a chord. Been doing that since I was three, but this time—WOOONGG. Never heard my guitar sound like that! As the sound bounces off the walls of the nearly empty arena, I can't help but think of all the dive bars I've played—horrible acoustics, microphones that smell like cigarettes and sweat, amps with feedback, people spilling beer. Now, here I am just *tuning*, and every note comes out crisp and strong. Man, it's been a long road to get here. Yeah, we're just the opening act, but this is *Chicago,* and this is the *United Center!*

My dad comes into my head. He spent 30 years playing places big and small, just to die when he was in his 40s. I feel a part of him is with me now. *Dad, I wish you could see this place.*

I look behind me, and I sense the energy in Crash and Billy as they set up. It's mic check time, and it's just like with the guitar. The sound is perfect. I stroll around the stage, gently strumming, going over the four songs we're gonna play. I know some guys would be about to puke at a time like this, but I'm filled with a surge of energy. This is my passion. This is what I do.

Time flies by. I look back and get nods from Billy and Crash. I can tell that all of their fright is gone. They're pumped and ready! The sound guys give me the thumbs up. Time to rock.

This DJ from a Chicago radio station bounces onto the stage. "Welcome to the March Rock Fest!" After a few shameless plugs, he gets down to business. "Ladies and gentlemen, please welcome—" he pauses for effect "—our opening act, from St. Louis, Missouri—" he pauses again, and my heart is pounding, "—here they are, The Dukes."

Here we go!

I feel a rush as I step to the mic. "Hello, Chicago!" You know, I *always* wanted to say that. Crash starts beatin' on the skins, and we're rockin.'

In an instant, all worries are gone. As a musician, I can tell when things are right. Can't explain it, I just *know* it, and right now, our sound is tight, and the adrenaline is flowing.

My eyes find Sheila on the floor in the front row. What a sight! She's jumping up and down, joy filling that beautiful face. It's kinda wild. I've only known her for a couple of weeks, but, damn, I feel connected. Seems like I'm singing directly to her.

We finish the first song with confidence. I imagine 20,000 people going wild, but in reality, there's only maybe a couple thousand people in the building. After all, we're just the first band with 14 more to follow.

But I don't care. Crash hits the drums again, and we roll into song number two. We slow it down with a mellow ballad for tune number three, then we're ready to finish big. When we make it to the radio, this one's gonna be the song that pops first. I *know* it.

So we rock into it, and we're feeling it, and I try to find Sheila's eyes. Well, she's there and she's dancing, but I'm shocked to see she's got a partner. It's *Oscar!* What the—? How'd he get—? But there he is—wearing his overalls. Bright, *yellow* overalls.

Well, we keep on rockin,' and Sheila and Oscar keep on dancing. *Man,* are they dancing. Others are bobbin' their heads, but Sheila and Oscar are *feeling* it. They've never heard this song, but they're dancing like it's their all-time favorite. I get a final surge from it all and finish with a flourish.

I thank the crowd, throw Sheila a smile, and we exit the stage. There's no way I can describe what it's like to hear a crowd still cheering when you're no longer in sight. I'm totally flying.

I know that I've been blessed with talent. I know that I can make it, and I know I'm closer than ever. I high-five Billy and Crash. "Guys, all I can say is 'Yeeeaaahhh!'"

———————— ♪ o 𝄪 ————————

Backstage, I run into Jenkins. As usual, his mouth is going. "Not bad, Manny. Knew this would be a good spot for you."

I'm feeling too good right now to let *anything* he says bother me.

"Yeah, Manny kid, this is the way I do it. I put people in position to succeed."

"Jenkins, you put *yourself* in position to *go to the bank*. Unlike us."

I lose focus on Jenkins as Sheila comes rushing up. To say I'm pleasantly surprised when she kisses me, well, you know what I mean. It's a big kiss, right on my sweaty, salty lips.

"Manny, you were great! Loved it! Wow!"

For a second, it feels like the two of us are alone.

"Hey, man—great show!" It ain't the voice of Jenkins.

"Oscar! How'd *you* get here?"

"I heard The Dukes were playing, man. I *had* to be here."

What I meant was, how did he get backstage, but I let

it go. Pretty cool he made the trip up here. We need fans. And certainly in one way, Oscar's our *biggest* fan. Plenty of girth inside those overalls. I stare at him, and he's got this look on his face. Hard to describe. The guy's just—happy. Really, really happy.

"Manny, I was praying for you, man."

Praying? "I thought you were dancing."

Oscar laughs. "You *thought* I was dancing? You didn't see me *groovin'?* You have your eyes closed up there?"

Now I'm laughing. He was groovin' for sure.

"Manny, I was praying and dancing at the same time. It ain't hard to do, brother."

While I was trying to process that, Sheila joins in. "Manny, I *wasn't* praying while I was dancing, but you know those prayers I said for you yesterday? Well, sure looks like they were answered. You were fantastic!"

I guzzle some water and smile. "Yeah. It sure felt good."

I leave Sheila and Oscar to go change my shirt. When I come back, Oscar's gone. Perfect. I ain't dating Mr. Overalls. So Sheila and I walk around the arena and take in a couple of the other bands. I love it when she says, "Manny, these guys can't compare to you!" I'm trying to work on humility, but you know, she's damn right.

We're starving—well, at least *I'm* starving. Are shapely girls like Sheila ever starving? Anyway, I'm figuring she's at least *hungry,* so I ask her if she knows any good places for grub.

"Sure."

A cab takes us a few miles south. We get out in front of this place called the Bongo Room. I'm a little confused. "Sheila, what the hell is this? This ain't no time for bongos. I gotta eat."

"I understand, silly. Wait 'til you see the menu in here."

Well, as usual, she's right. The place has all kinds of wild stuff. I order the pancakes. But they're not *just* pancakes here. The menu reads: 'Ground red cornmeal hotcakes with powdered sugar, fresh cranberries, topped with toasted pecan, honey, and bourbon butter.'

"What are you getting, Sheila?"

"Mmm, I think the Vegetarian Croissant Sandwich."

The veggie? How boring. Then I read what's on it: 'Muenster, spinach, tomatoes, sautéed mushrooms, cucumber, alfalfa sprouts, scallions, one egg, basil. Served with potatoes.' Yum.

"Manny, I'm not just saying this. You are *really* talented."

"Hey, I told you that I played on stage the first time we met. You doubted me?"

"Well, no, but guys throw all kinds of lines at me, and they're not always telling the truth." She laughs. "When I was 18, this guy told me he played for the New York Yankees. And I believed him."

I hide a laugh behind my napkin. "You *believed* him?"

"Well, yeah, he was hot and athletic and—"

"Who woke you up?"

She smiles. "My dad. He and I went shopping and we ran into the guy. My dad's been a Yankees fan for decades, and he knew in a New York minute this guy was a fraud."

74

I'm laughing. "Any guy ever tell you he was an astronaut?"

"Stop it. I'm not *always* gullible."

"You weren't so sure about me."

"Well, I wasn't *sure*. I mean, nobody had ever told me they were going to be a rock star." She smiles. "But after this morning, I'm sure you're the real deal, Manny."

If there's anyone I want to hear that from, it's her.

"Manny, let me ask you this—did you write those songs?"

"Yep. I love to write. I've got tons of songs in my head. It may take a while, Sheila, but someday a lot of my songs are gonna be out there."

"How long's the process? How's it all work?"

I sigh. I don't know. "Well, part of music is a business, and I don't understand the business. That's what Jenkins is for, to figure all this stuff out, but I'm not sure he can get the job done."

"Jenkins?" She frowns. "Yuck. I don't like that guy."

"Well, let's not talk about him."

Fortunately, the food at the Bongo Room makes it easy to forget Jenkins. As we're eating, Sheila says that we should go visit the Art Institute. If she said we should go jump off a bridge, I'd say okay. Inside, I'm feeling the warm ember of this morning's performance coupled with the companionship of this special, beautiful woman who is so easy and fun to be with. Did I just say that? She's bringing out the poetry in me.

By the way, the pancakes are unforgettable.

When we step out onto the street, we're blasted by the chill of the March wind. We're about 10 steps from the restaurant when we hear a voice.

"Hey, you two lovers. Can you help me?"

Lovers? We look down and see a man sitting on the cold sidewalk, bundled up against the wind. He's only got one leg. He's wrapped in a heavy sweatshirt stained with who knows what. He's sporting what's probably a three-day beard.

"How 'bout a little money to help me get on the bus?"

I look at Sheila who is already looking at me. Before I can say anything, the guy on the sidewalk says, "You two look really good together." We look to him, and then back to each other, and I'm wondering, 'what do we do?'

So Sheila asks him, "How much is the bus?"

"Well, 10 bucks will get me *on* the bus, *and* a meal when I get home."

Sheila asks me, "What do you think?"

Man, I wish she didn't do that. I don't know. I just shrug.

Sheila whips her billfold out of her purse, and gives the guy a 10.

"Thank you, Miss. You are very pretty." Then he looks at me and says, "And you're a very lucky guy."

We walk in silence for a minute. I ask her, "Do you think he's really going to buy a meal?"

She pauses for a moment. "No way of knowing, Manny, unless we get on the bus and follow him home. These cases are tough, but I usually err on the side of charity."

———————— ♪ o ♭ ————————

It feels great to be inside the Art Institute after our 15-minute walk in the chill. We immediately cruise through a couple of the major exhibits. I don't know about you, but I'm not the kind of guy who stands in front of a painting for so long that he has to take a pee, and I'm glad to discover that Sheila's the same way. We decide to go to the museum café for some java.

"So Manny, tell me more about your band."

I chuckle. Wow. I mean, fair question, actually an obvious question, but how do I explain Crash and Billy?

"Well, one funny thing is, Billy outweighs Crash by more than 200 pounds."

"Right. I have eyes. Tell me how you found them."

"I got lucky with Crash. Put up fliers at a few record stores, and he answered the call. He came over to our house to audition. When I asked him his name, and he said, 'Crash,' I thought, hmm, this guy's got some *potential*. Well, he sat down at Lenny's old drum kit and just killed it. I asked him when he could start. He told me 'whenever, dude.'"

Sheila smiles.

"The thing about Crash is, when he's not behind the drums, you can barely tell he's got a pulse, but when he gets those sticks in his hands, he explodes."

Sheila nods. "You got that right. I thought he was great! And what about Billy?"

"I saw him playing with another band and he was so good he was stealing the show. Pretty rare for a bassist. A couple weeks later I saw that band again, but Billy wasn't there. I asked the front-man where he was and he said, 'Gone. Drugs.'"

So I ask the guy, "'What? He's *dead*?'"

"No, but he's close," the guy says. "We couldn't take it anymore and we had to lose him."

I take a sip of my coffee. "Well, I knew I had to find this guy. Maybe it was because of the way my dad died, or maybe I just needed an amazing bassist. So I get his number and give him a call.

"It's a long story, but after a couple of meetings I get serious about his issue. I tell him, 'Listen, man, my dad is in his grave right now because of this same exact shit. You got talent and you can help me make something great here. But you gotta get clean.'"

Sheila puts her hands around her almost empty coffee cup, and looks concerned. "Wow. Is he sober now?"

"He's been in and out of rehab, but lately he's been doing really well. As far as I know, he hasn't touched the stuff in six months."

Sheila exhales. "I'll pray for him, Manny. He can really play."

"Yeah, you're not kidding. What Clarence Clemons was to the sax, Billy is to the bass."

I usually keep Billy's case private, but for some reason it feels good—and right—to share honestly with this girl. I feel like I could talk to her about anything.

We get a second cup of coffee, and she starts chatting about Steve and Rachel.

"Did you know they're going out tonight?"

Damn, these women. They share everything. Did I know Steve was going out tonight? Steve probably goes out *every* night. So I say, "Well, I'm not surprised. I know Steve's really attracted to her."

"Rachel's into him, too. Manny, just about every man is attracted to Rachel, but she's not interested in every man. She's pretty excited about Steve."

Now, I could say every woman is attracted to Steve, and he *is interested* in just about every woman. Or, at least in sleeping with them. But I can't say that. "Well, we'll see what happens."

After we finish the second cup, we head out. Sheila goes to Granny's, I go to the hotel, and we agree to meet later that night. No doubt my cab driver's wondering about the smile on my face. It's been a great day, and I have a feeling this is gonna be a *very* special evening.

10

♩.♪ *In the swirl of life,*
 I'm feeling the breeze,
 Gonna keep on movin',
  won't you help me, please?
 Won't you help me, please! ♪ 𝅗𝅥·

"Swirl of Life"
— The Dukes (Manny Morrison)

So, we're sitting in this romantically lit dining room off State Street. Sheila's wearing a cream silk blouse, covered by a cool jacket. I'm no fashion designer, so I can't analyze all the threads. But I know it looks classy, and I know I like it. Down below, she's wearing a skirt, which gives me my first look at her legs. They're nice. *Really* nice.

In this lighting, she looks, I don't know, I don't throw around words like "glamorous" and "fabulous," but I really don't know what else to say. She doesn't need much makeup, and since I don't work for Max Factor, I can't tell you what she's wearing, but whatever it is, it's perfect.

Now, I *can* give you something about her features. Her lips are round and full with a softness to them, the kind I could kiss all night. Her hair looks better than ever, and I'm thinking, man, Granny must have given her some great shampoo. Love her earrings. Heart-shaped studs. But, the thing that *really* gets me—and this is every time I see her—is her eyes. Never seen a girl with such dark hair and such light, crystal clear blue eyes. She's the whole package.

Anyway, the name of the restaurant is Osteria Via Stato. Certified Italiano. The atmosphere is perfect.

Sheila quickly decides to have the seafood stew. I scan the menu and I see "Chicken Mario"—inspired by Chef Mario of Sostanza in Florence. I'm goin' with Chef Mario.

I figure we'll go someplace later for alcohol, so to save a few bucks, we order a cheap bottle of wine. At least, cheap for the standards of the ol' Osteria.

"So, tell me, Manny—do you have any tattoos?"

Man, this girl never holds back. Whatever she wants to know, she just spews, and I've got no choice but to answer. But you know, I kind of like that. I hate those girls who beat around the bush. Or, just sit there and stare and say nothing so you can't tell if they're thinking about you, or their lipstick, or nothing at all.

"No tats."

"Really? None?"

"None. I stay away from needles."

"Ahh," she says, nodding. "Your dad—"

"Yeah, he made me wish I'd never seen a needle." Don't wanna get going on that subject. "Okay, how about you? You a tatted lady?"

"I guess I could be."

"You got some hidden away?"

"I could have."

"Well, do you?"

"That's for you to find out."

Well, that's gonna be fun. "So, you got any more, deep, personal questions?"

She smiles as if she's got a million. "Have you ever kissed a girl?"

I crack up. I'm trying to think of something witty. "Well, I kissed you, right?"

"No. I kissed *you.* Twice. Yesterday at Willis Tower, and today backstage."

Well, at this second, I'm thinking about climbing across the table and thrilling her with my "first kiss," but I notice the maître d' is keeping an eye on us. "Sheila, I'm biding my time. Waiting for the perfect moment." I give her this knowing look, and she smiles. A great time to clink our wine glasses.

"Okay, girl, what else?"

"Um, I want to know…" she pauses, which kills me, "…what's the craziest thing you've ever done?"

Mentally, I start going through my list. The craziest thing—no, can't tell her that. The second craziest—uh-unh, no way. Number three—nah, can't go with that. Well, let's see—oh!

"Well, I probably shouldn't be telling you this—" teasing her, of course—"but one night after a gig, Billy and Crash and I all get a little drunk. Well, Billy's not a little drunk. He's totally drunk. We're on Washington Avenue, and it's a Friday night, and there are these bikers who have ridden into town. Well, somehow, one of the guys' bikes winds up on the ground, and he accuses Billy of knocking it over. Billy tells him he doesn't know what he's talking about, and all of a sudden, three bikers jump on Billy. Well, back in college, Billy's nickname was 'The One-Man Riot Squad.' He starts throwing these guys around, and almost like children, they pick up their bikes and go home. But Billy's so drunk, he's looking for the next fight. Well, there's about six guys watching this, and Billy starts trash talking. He calls them 'sissies' in about nine different ways.

"Well, Crash and I know this is trouble. We don't want these guys associating *us* with *him*. No need to get beat up by proxy. I step between Billy and the bikers. 'I'll take care of this, fellas.' Well, there's no way words are gonna convince Billy to cool it, so I tackle him."

Sheila's eyes grow wide.

"Or, at least I try to. Remember he was throwing three guys around just a second ago, and they were bigger than me. Skinny little Crash just looks scared to death, and I know he's not gonna be any help. I know I need to get creative. So I sneak behind Billy and pull his legs out from under him as hard as I can. He would have landed on his face, but his belly is so big it holds his head safely off the ground."

Sheila chuckles. I can hardly believe I'm telling her this story.

"Well, we roll him over on his back just as this cop shows up. He looks at Billy, then he looks at me. 'Hey! You know this guy?'

"'Never seen him before in my life, officer.'"

Sheila is laughing.

"Well, just *one* cop has no chance of moving Billy, so he calls an EMT. It almost takes a crane, but they get him on a stretcher and put him in an ambulance. The cop won't tell me where they're taking him because 'I don't know the guy.'

"Well, I'm not too proud of this—" I pause to sip my wine "—but I wanted to see where they were taking my friend, and I see this bicycle, unlocked, and I jump on it. I'm pedaling like a madman chasing the ambulance when a car pulls out from a side street. I slam into it and get thrown over the top.

"Long story short, I end up in the same hospital where they took Billy. I'm in the waiting room for a couple hours. By that time, Billy's sober and on the way out. He's shocked to see me. 'Man, what the hell happened to *you*?'"

Sheila's laughing out loud. She picks up her wine glass and proposes a toast. "To loyal and concerned friends everywhere."

Ah, now it's her turn. Looking forward to this. "And—your craziest?"

Sheila puts her hand to her chin. I'm wondering if she's going through *her* 'mental list.' Looks like it.

"So, it happened at the end of a work day at St. Vincent de Paul. Rachel and I are about to leave the office—"

"Wait a minute. Rachel works with you?"

"Yep." I'm really surprised, but I let her go on. "Rachel started at SVDP before me. Anyway, a client named Terrell is with us. When he was two, he fell down a flight of stairs while his dad was on drugs. So, he's developmentally disabled. He's 28, but mentally he's about eight. Sweetest guy in the world. We call him 'the friendliest man in North America.'

"Well, Terrell's group home has asked if we can drive him home. We ask if 7 o'clock is okay, as Rachel and I are going to meet some friends at The Rock House and Terrell wants to come along. So, Happy Hour is in full swing when we get there. Now, you gotta know Terrell. Mr. Spontaneous. Rachel and I are holding sodas when Terrell announces, 'I can walk on my hands.' And with that, he puts his hands to the floor, and starts moving. Sadly, his foot smacks this guy right in the face."

I start laughing. "That's hilarious."

"Well, if you were there, it wouldn't seem so funny. I mean, he inadvertently kicks this guy *right in the face.*"

I'm laughing louder now. Some things just strike me as funny.

Sheila smiles and shakes her head. "The guy looks at Terrell, who by now has his feet back on the floor, and I think he's gonna kill him. So, Rachel and I run over to the guy and try to calm him down. We listen until he gets done cursing and swearing, and then we explain that we work for SVDP and that Terrell is our client. Despite the four-letter words, he seems like a man of means. He starts asking about the St. Vincent de Paul Society, and Rachel and I are only too happy to fill him in. One thing leads to another, and after we take Terrell home, we agree to meet the guy at his country club. I won't bore you with the details, but after he treats us to dinner—and hears a couple of hours' worth of stories about the clients we serve—he writes St. Vincent de Paul a check for $50,000."

My jaw drops. "Wow! That's incredible."

"Yep. It was our biggest donation of the entire year."

I shake my head and smile. I'm the kind of guy who can get bored pretty easily on a date, but it ain't gonna happen with this girl. I mean, tats, kisses, kicks to the face, a $50,000 check. I'm wide awake—and having fun.

So we eat this scrumptious dinner—yep, Chef Mario came through—and I suggest we go for drinks.

"Manny, I know a cool place for that."

At this point, I'd follow her anywhere.

——————— ♪ o ♭ ———————

Twenty minutes later, me and Sheila are in the Signature Lounge, on the 95th floor of the Hancock Tower. The lights of the city shine for miles, offset by the black appearance of Lake Michigan at night. Soft jazz wafts through the hidden speakers of a high-quality sound system. We sit at a cozy little table right by the window. I feel like I could write about five new love songs if I had my guitar.

We each order a "Specialty Cocktail." Sheila gets "Peaches in Paris" while I opt for the "Skyscraper." The drinks are great. The "Specialty Price," uh, not so much. Sixteen bucks a drink!

"Manny, don't you love this place?"

"I love being here with you."

For a couple of seconds we just look into each other's eyes. After a few sips, I can't hold back. I slowly lean forward. Our lips meet. To me, this is the first kiss that counts. The others were such a surprise that I didn't have much time to enjoy them. But here, there's no reason to rush. We start to pull apart, but I slowly dive in for one more.

I pull back and we look at each other. Her face is radiant. I mean, it's *glowing*. I'm feeling electric.

"Let's get back to the hotel."

I see her lean back. I try to act cool.

"What would we do there?"

"What would we do? Uh…Sheila I really like you—"

"I like you, too, Manny."

"I'd like to wrap my arms around you."

"And?"

"And—spend the night."

I see a look of concern, so I say, "We can stop off and feed the cats before we go."

Sheila shakes her head. "Manny, this isn't about the cats. I can't spend the night with you."

"Huh? Why? You didn't like my kisses?"

She hesitates. "No, Manny your kisses were great." A small smile forms on her lips. "Really great, actually."

Well, I'm feeling good about that.

She leans toward me, lowers her voice, and in the most endearing tone, she says, "Manny, I think it'd be really great to wait until marriage."

Huh? Really great? What?!? "Uh, Sheila, uh, I think it's way too early to start talkin' about marriage—" I see her nodding. "But in the meantime, this is a way we could get closer, and you know how great it is to—"

She cuts me off. "Not exactly, Manny. I'm a virgin."

A *virgin?* Is she kidding? I've had a lot surprises in my life, but this has gotta rank in the top five. Maybe the top three.

"You're kidding, right?" She's shaking her head, no. "Sheila, you really surprise me." I let out a long, slow breath. And then I think of something. "You mentioned that you were Catholic. If that's the reason, I've been with—I mean I've talked to—lots of Catholic girls and, uh, this hasn't come up before."

She leans in closer. "Manny, this is about doing what is *right.* Now, I want you to know that I really like you. And there's a whole lot to like. I mean, today has been *wonderful.* But if this is a problem for you, well, I don't know what to say."

I'm shocked. I'm stunned. I can't believe this is happening. This has been one of the greatest days of my life, and now this?

"Sheila, you *really* surprised me. Um, I'm going to have to think about this. I don't know what else to say except that I think you're special. Very special. And I don't want this to end."

"It's been quite a day, Manny. Maybe it's time we both go and get some rest."

CHAPTER

11

♪ *I'm cruisin' today, gonna make my way,*
  No worries and lies,
  just burgers and fries. ♪ **o·**

"Burgers and Fries"
— The Dukes (Billy Wilkinson)

On Monday morning, I'm home alone, lounging on the red leather wrap-around. My head's still spinning over Sheila. If she's into me as much as I think she is, I just don't get what the holdup is. I scratch my head. Boy, life is moving fast. I mean, I meet Sheila *just 15 days ago.* And *one day later,* I luck into a friendship with the richest wide receiver in NFL history.

Then, Saturday—well, Saturday's pace is totally off the charts. We rock the *United Center,* then I get to spend the rest of the day with Sheila. I just sorta thought the way things were headed I was gonna spend the rest of the night with her too. Instead the night ends with this bomb dropping over cocktails 95 floors up. I gotta get out of the house.

I meet Steve at Five Star Burgers after his morning

workout. Want to tell him about the concert and the *experience* with Sheila, and I gotta see what happened with him and Rachel.

We both order the "Breakfast of Champions" burger. It's topped with a sunny side up egg, American cheese, roasted tomato-bacon jam, and hollandaise.

"So, buddy, tell me about the Rock Fest."

"It went great, man. Played four songs, all originals, and the crowd was into it. Biggest stage we've ever played. Sound system was amazing. The band was tight. Couldn't have gone any better."

Steve looks happy for me. "Tremendous. I was thinking how that concert would have been like my first preseason game, rookie year. I was scared shitless, but it all went well, and before long, I became Mr. Six. So the crowd was good, huh?"

I can't keep from smiling. "Well, the best-*looking* person in the crowd was Sheila. She was groovin' right in front of the stage. It was great to watch her move. The big shock was who she was dancing with."

Steve gives me a little grin. "Who? Michael Jordan?"

"Not exactly. It was Oscar."

"Oscar?" Steve raises his eyebrows. "You mean, Overalls Oscar?"

"Yep. Wearing yellow 'ralls. Must be his concert get-up."

"Did you know he was coming?"

"Had no idea. Didn't tell him we were playing. Next thing I know, he was with us backstage."

"How'd he get back there?"

"I don't know." And then something hit me. "You know, he said he *had* to come, that he wasn't gonna miss The Dukes."

"So, he's a fan of the band. Maybe he saw you at the Pageant."

I think about the possibility for a second. "Yeah, but then why didn't he recognize me when we were at Kaldi's—and when we were at brunch?"

Steve throws up his hands. "Man, I don't know." For a second we just look at each other, then he moves on. "So anyway, how did it go with Sheila?"

"Well, it was pretty amazing. Her Granny lives up there, so she really knows Chi-town. She was taking me to all kinds of places. The Art Institute, the Willis Tower, a couple of cool restaurants. We wound up 95 stories up in the Hancock Tower for drinks. Little table with a great view of the city."

"Nice. Sounds intimate. How was the hotel?"

"Kinda dumpy. Nothin' special."

"No, I mean, how was it with Sheila?"

"Well, she didn't come back with me."

Steve frowns. "She didn't come back with you? Why not? You couldn't seal the deal?"

"No, it's not like that, man. It's just—." I pause. I don't know what he's gonna think about this. I lower my voice. "She told me she's a virgin."

Steve starts chuckling. I wonder why he's responding like that. Then he says, "Wow, that's kinda how it went with Rachel, too."

I almost choke on my burger. "*Rachel's* a virgin?"

"Uh, no. But just about. She told me she had sex with one guy, one time, and she's sorry she did it."

I'm all but speechless. Sheila and Rachel, two fabulously gorgeous women—bright, cool, fun. I never would have guessed that they wouldn't be willing—. "So, Steve, what did you say?"

"Well, I asked her why she was sorry, and while she didn't go into detail, she told me the guy turned out to be a jerk. So, I told her that I wasn't a jerk, that it would be much different with me. But she said she was going to wait until she gets married."

I look down and shake my head. "Wow. I've got the same thing goin' on with Sheila. How'd you leave it with Rachel?"

Steve swallows a bite, and takes a drink. "Well, I told her that I really enjoyed our time together, but if we were never going to—well, I pretty much let her know I'd be going in a different direction." He pauses. "So, I assume you told Sheila pretty much the same thing?"

I gulp. I mean, I'm not planning on saying goodbye to Sheila just like that. After all, I've only known her for a couple of weeks, and maybe she'll change. "Not exactly. I'm hoping that Sheila comes around."

"Hey—you can't wait forever, buddy. A man's got needs."

12

~ *Sheila* ~

I'm pretty sure yesterday was like one of those romantic moments every girl dreams of. Manny is seriously not like any other guy I've met. He's so passionate and we just—*go* together. Even the people on the streets could see it. So why is it the only thing I can think about is how it ended? That look of disbelief. And *disappointment*. I mean, I did the right thing, right? So why am I so worried that he's not gonna call? I need to talk to Rachel. Maybe she can knock some sense into me over some coffee. We've got a *lot* to talk about.

Thirty minutes later, Rachel and I are sitting in the kitchen. "So, after telling me you were thinking about doing it with him, you told Manny that you won't?" Rachel asks, as she puts some more sweetener in her coffee and returns the box to the pantry.

"Well, I told him it'd be great to wait until marriage, and that I was a virgin, and that this could be an issue. That's what I told *him*—but I could still change my mind, right?"

"Well, not if Manny blows you off. Do you think he's still gonna want to go out with you?"

"Rachel, what can I say? I don't know. I know for sure that I surprised him. I mean, he looked *totally* surprised. But he didn't get crazy about it. Actually, he didn't say very much. Maybe I didn't let him. I told him we both should take off and get some rest."

"Well, you're a little luckier than me. Steve didn't get crazy, he just said in not so many words, 'It's been nice knowing you.'"

"What a jerk."

Rachel puts her coffee cup down and leans across the table. "Sheila, don't you dare tell anybody this—but I almost decided to sleep with him."

"Rachel, really?"

"Well, yeah. Sure he's good looking and everything, but he's more than that. He's funny and fun-loving and we really had a good time together. And, you know, when you're in that moment, it's hard to resist. It's hard to just *turn off* what your body is feeling even when your head is telling you no! Besides, just think if it all worked out—the kind of house we'd be living in, the places we'd go, the things we'd do."

Rachel leans back and sighs. "We all know Steve's a little weak, and sure, he's far from perfect, but I know I could be good for him."

"I guess I'm a little surprised to hear you say that—especially after what you told me about the Fraternity Prez. But I understand, Rachel. Steve's a rare dream, and in so many ways. But, really, do you think it'd be the right thing to do?"

Rachel sighs and chooses not to answer my question. "Sheila, you're so much stronger than me."

"Rachel, I'm weaker than you think."

13

♩ ♪ *Been down too long,*
  gotta leave this place,
 Gonna find my way,
  gonna end this chase. ♪ 𝅝·

"The Chase"
— The Dukes (Manny Morrison)

So I get back to my house after lunch with Steve, and I'm half thinkin' about what the hell to do about Sheila, and half thinkin' about the next move for The Dukes when I get a call from a number I don't recognize.

"Manny, this is Wally Wallace."

I'm trying to process. "Wally Wallace? Do I know you?"

"No. But I know enough about *you.* Saw you play Saturday in Chicago. You need me, Manny."

"I do, huh?" I ask, pouring in the skepticism. Who the hell is *this* guy?

"Well, let me correct myself. You don't *need* me, Manny. You've got talent, and you're going to do nothing but play music the rest of your life. You're good. Real good. I think you have a chance to become great. But the way your career is managed, starting *right now,* can make all the difference in the world. I'm a music guru. I manage artists. It's what I do. And I can help you *right now."*

I take a breath. Don't get calls like this every day, but still—. "If you're a manager, already got one. Sonny Jenkins."

"Right. Which is *precisely* why you need *me,* right now."

I still don't know who this guy is, but clearly he's not the president of the Sonny Jenkins Fan Club. "Can you go a little deeper here, Mr. Guru?"

"Sure. Would love to. That's why I came into St. Louis. Flew in just to see you, Manny. Let's talk over dinner. How about we meet at Mia Sorella, terrific restaurant, on me. 7 o'clock. Sound good?"

Free meals always sound good. And hey, can't hurt to listen. "Sure. See you then."

Well, Wally's right about Mia Sorella. Terrific place. He's got us set up in a private booth in the back. Nice.

I'm surprised that he's so young. Hearing him on the phone, I figured he was about 50. Deep authoritative voice, convincing speech. But he looks like he's about 35. In contrast to Jenkins, he has a look of class. Gold wedding band. Neatly trimmed hair. Nice tan, but not so deep that he looks like he's coming in from South Beach. I ask where he *is* coming in from.

"Chicago. Remember I was there on Saturday? My company, Wallace Management, has offices in Chicago and L.A."

It doesn't take long for Wally to get down to business. I like that. Can't stand it when people start talking about the weather when you know damn well that they want something.

"Manny, how many people would you say know about The Dukes?"

"Well, there's people in St. Louis who have heard me. We did a gig a couple of weeks ago at the Pageant—"

"Outside of St. Louis."

"Um, not too many."

"Yeah. We're going to change that."

"*We* are?"

"Let me tell you what I do. I'm not a booking agent, but I've got connections. I'm not a recording studio, but again, I've got connections. Very strong connections. What I do is direct and manage careers."

"Which means what?"

He gets a look on his face as if I asked him to change my diaper. "Let's see, where should I start? Do you have a good photo of your band?"

"Well, this girl I knew in college took the picture you saw in the program up in Chicago."

"Right. We can do better."

"You a photographer?"

"No. But I have one. And believe it or not, she's *a little bit better* than your college friend. She's the best. What's your first album cover look like?"

"Well, we don't have one. We haven't—"

"Well, you're going to need one. We do that. We do

tremendous graphics. What label are you going to record on?"

"Don't know yet. See, we're still putting together the last cuts for—"

"You ever hear of Jupiter Records?"

Jupiter? Did he just say, *Jupiter?* "Well, yeah, sure. Everyone has. They've come out of nowhere to be—huge."

Wally nods knowingly. "Right. My older brother is their CEO."

I'm stunned into silence.

"Manny, that's the label we'll be recording on."

"We *will?*"

"Manny, let me be direct. My greatest gift is identifying people who are good enough to make it. That's my job. See, when it comes to knocking out CDs in my brother's studio, each one takes weeks. And lots and lots of money. We're in the business of launching careers, but if the talent isn't there, well, it doesn't work so well, and my brother loses a lot of dough. So, he trusts me to find new artists who are good. Damn good. What I saw of you in Chicago convinced me that you and your skinny ass drummer and the fat bass guy—well, you've got a chance."

Now, with the way things have been moving the last couple of weeks, I shouldn't be surprised that Mr. Music Guru is zipping right along here. Still, I feel like calling a timeout. But he's forging ahead.

"I saw you play four songs up there. Originals, right?"

"Yep."

"You wrote 'em?"

"All of them."

"Impressive. How many more have you written?"

"Man, I've got *notebooks* full of songs, but there's four more special ones that we've honed, and I'm working hard on about eight others."

"Okay. So, we've got the four I heard, plus the four you're tight with. We only need four more before we record, so choose the best four out of the other eight, and blast away on those."

"Sounds good." Whoa, what am I saying? Well, it *does* sound good, almost too good to be true. But what's the deal? Am I jumping too fast here? I feel excited, but I'm still a little suspicious.

Well, we talk for a couple hours over dinner, and my concerns disappear. Wally opens up and tells me how his genius brother made mega-millions as an IT wizard, and how he couldn't stand the state of the music biz, so he founded Jupiter Records to fix it. Then he tells me how his big bro sent him out on the road to find a few new groups, and how, with a few smart moves, it all mushroomed into the hottest label in the world.

I don't know, it's kinda hard to explain, but I just come to trust the guy. I feel *good* about him. *Comfortable.* And maybe the drinks help.

Anyway, I gotta tell you that when I get to feeling comfortable with somebody, I like to do fun things, like, make up nicknames and stuff.

So toward the end of dinner, I tell Wally that they should call him, Wally "Waldo" Wallace. I don't know why, it just hits me as funny. Well, he doesn't exactly laugh his butt off or anything, but he soaks it in pretty well. Me, I'm proud of myself. Wally "Waldo" Wallace is one cool name. And I agree to let him manage The Dukes. Which means—I gotta fire Jenkins.

———————— ♪ o 𝄻 ————————

The next day I'm sipping a cup of java with Jenkins at Denny's. I've got no reason to beat around the bush.

"Sonny, nothing stays the same in this world, and, uh, I've decided to hire someone else to represent me."

I can see Jenkins wasn't expecting this. "You *what?*"

"Look, Sonny, it's time for The Dukes to move on."

He slams his fists on the table. "Manny, after all I've done for you—"

"Like what, Sonny? The Pageant? Yeah, Chicago was good, but you gave me about 10 minutes' notice, and we played for free. And that's it, after two-and-a-half years?"

"Manny, we're just starting to roll here! You killed it in Chicago, and from here, we're headin' straight up."

Well, I'm heading straight up, but I ain't bringing Jenkins along for the ride. "Jenkins, after all this time, we've got no CD, no merchandizing—"

"Manny, I'm going to get you recording soon. You know I've been a little busy, but now—"

"Sonny, there's no reason to go on with this. My agreement with you says you get a big fat percentage of every gig you book for us, after expenses. What I'm saying is, we don't need you to book anything else."

101

"Manny, I can't believe this! You're nothin' but a punk. You think this business is easy? I'll tell you right now—you're goin' nowhere without me, asshole. You'll see."

And with that, he gets up and storms out.

Well, you know what I'm thinkin'? That's the last time I'm ever gonna have to look at *that damn plaid sport coat*. Good riddance.

CHAPTER

14

♩.♪ *I keep lookin' for the answers,*
keep lookin' for the light,
I'm gonna leave this darkness,
get it out of sight,
At least I think I might. ♪ o·

"Lookin' for the Light"
— The Dukes (Manny Morrison)

"Manny, this is so exciting!"

Sheila and I are sipping decaf later that night at Kaldi's.

I can't keep from babbling. "Jupiter Records! And my new man, Waldo. He's a far cry from Jenkins. And all I got to do is hone these last four songs, and we're gonna have a CD. Sheila, I always thought my first would be on a label like Hogwash Vinyls, but we're gonna debut on *Jupiter*. We gotta celebrate."

"Love to, Manny." Her smile almost makes the coffee sizzle.

"How about Saturday night. I'm thinking of this place—"

"Oh, Manny, I'm sorry. Rachel and I have to be at this

103

fundraiser for St. Vincent de Paul Saturday night."

I'm feeling a little crushed.

"But—" she says with a wink, "I'd *love* to celebrate with you on Sunday morning at brunch. Right after 10 a.m. Mass!"

I sigh. I try to withhold some of my exasperation, but my idea of celebration isn't exactly brunch after *Mass.* But what can I do? I gotta see her. We gotta celebrate. There's nobody else I'd rather celebrate with.

"So, let's see, you go to Mass, and then we meet somewhere at a hot brunch spot?"

"No, silly. You go to Mass *with* me, and we could go somewhere afterwards together."

Oh, brother. "Sheila, I don't know if I can do that."

"Sure, you can."

"Well, I know I *can.* I just don't really want to."

"Manny, Manny, Manny. I know you're kind of out of the routine, but I'm sure it will all come back to you. Besides, I really want to introduce you to one of my friends, one of our priests."

This is going from bad to worse. Meet a priest. *A priest!* Like I need some old guy, wearing a collar, hitting me over the head with his Bible.

"Come on, Manny. Just come and meet him. We'll chat for a couple of minutes after Mass, and then we'll head to brunch."

It's not worth an argument. So I agree to meet Father Waste-My-Time on Sunday, but I don't know how long I can take this Catholic stuff.

Five days later, I'm standing outside the Cathedral Basilica. Here comes Sheila. In a dress. A very cool dress. An unbuttoned sweater covers her shoulders. Perfect for an early April day.

Meanwhile, I'm wearing a sweater with my jeans. She walks in and I follow her. She goes about halfway down the aisle and genuflects. I remember doing that when I was a kid. Should I do it now? Eh, I just follow her into the pew.

Can't deny this church is beautiful. *Stunningly beautiful.* Mosaic images of Jesus and the saints are everywhere. Let's see, that must be St. Peter over there, but I wouldn't want to be quizzed on the rest. I can barely make out the sayings on the walls. I'm guessing they're Bible passages or something.

Before Mass begins, Sheila's kneeling and praying. I'm sitting and reflecting. As I told Sheila, I used to go to Mass with Mom. My dad, on the other hand, only went to Mass twice—on the day of his wedding and on the day of Mom's funeral.

Well, the Mass starts, and as I was expecting, the priest is about a hundred years old. Well, maybe about 70, but you know what I mean. We stand, we sit, we listen to the readings. Well, it comes time for the homily, and I don't want to fall asleep on Sheila, so I'm hoping this guy is interesting.

He starts out, "My dear brothers and sisters in Christ. Today's Gospel has always captivated me. Our Lord says in Luke, 'Every hair on your head has been counted.' I have heard that the average blonde has 150,000 hairs—"

Hmm. Gone out with my share of blondes, but I never counted.

"—the average brunette has 125,000 hairs—"

I glance at Sheila and start to count. I get to about 10. Don't know what the exact number is, but all of hers are beautiful.

"—and the average redhead has about 100,000. Isn't it amazing that God knows us better than we know ourselves? You see, God knows *everything* about us. This tells us that *God loves us.* So, tomorrow, when you comb your hair, remember that God knows how many you have up there—and remember to give Him praise."

Wow, that was different. What the hell do *I* think about when I comb *my* hair?

Anyway, the Mass continues, everyone says the Our Father—I remember that one—and it comes time for Communion. I watch as Sheila and several hundred others approach the altar. Some people look distracted, but I can't help but notice the look of peace and reverence on the faces of some of the others as they come back to their pews.

A few minutes later, the priest blesses everybody, the choir sings the final song, and we head for the door.

Well, we leave the main part of the church, and I'm figuring this is where I'm going to meet the old priest, Sheila's friend. But as I approach him, Sheila grabs my hand and pulls me over to the left.

"Manny, I'd like you to meet my friend, Father Max."

I'm stunned. *This* dude's standing there in a Roman collar, but he doesn't look like any priest I've ever seen. I'm guessing he's no older than 30. I'm 6'2" and he's looking me right in the eye. He looks like he could go and lift weights with Steve. He must have broken a lot of hearts when he went into the seminary.

"How are ya, Father?"

Before he can answer, Sheila jumps in and says, "Father, Manny and I are going to brunch. Would you like to join us?"

Whoa, hold on. That wasn't my plan. But Sheila's being Sheila again. Of course, the priest says yes, that he'll meet us in a few minutes after he chats with the faithful.

Twenty minutes later, we're sitting inside a place called Crepes, Etc.

The outgoing Father Max opens with, "So, Manny, what do you do?"

Guess Sheila hasn't told him anything about me. "I'm a musician."

Sheila interrupts. "Father, Manny's a *fabulous* musician. In fact, we're celebrating his gig in Chicago, and his new agent."

The Padre's eyes light up. "Nice. I love music! What kind of music do you play?"

He would probably love it if I said the viola. "Uh, Father, I play rock. I write my own stuff. Maybe not your style."

Father Max starts beaming. "I love *classic* rock. You?"

How about that? "Love it. My dad would be happy to hear you say that. He played that style his whole career. Actually, most of my songs have their roots in classic rock. Did you ever play, Father?"

Father leans back and smiles. "Not music." He chuckles. "I played football."

Football? "Where'd you play?"

"Notre Dame."

I lean forward. *"Notre Dame?!"*

The young priest laughs. "Yeah, but don't get too excited. I was a tall version of Rudy. A walk-on. Just played two years."

I'm still impressed. "Wow. Why'd you only play two years?"

"Well, I knew I'd never make it to the NFL—so I chucked the shoulder pads to figure out what I wanted to do."

I scratch my head. "So, this is it?" I say, pointing at his collar. "You probably could have done a lot of things. Why this?"

"Well, I came home to St. Louis for the summer after my sophomore year, and this priest, this fun-loving young guy at our parish, asked me, 'Have you ever thought about becoming a priest?' Well, I never had, but once he asked me, the question sort of stayed with me if you know what I mean. Long story short, I switched my major to theology, and here I am today."

I can't keep from asking, "Are you gay?"

"Manny!" Sheila shrieks.

"It's okay, Sheila." He glances at her then back at me. "No, I'm not."

"Have you ever had sex?"

"Manny! I can't believe you."

Father Max laughs. "Sheila, it's okay. I'm a pro at answering all kinds of questions. And I always answer honestly. No, Manny, I haven't, but it's not like I've never wanted to."

I think about that. "Wow. You must have a lot of self-control."

"Yes, and grace. I'm not saying it's always been easy. But the more you come to understand God's plan for human sexuality, the easier it is to know why sex is reserved for the married."

Well, I certainly disagree with the guy, but I can't help but wonder how he arrived at where he's at.

"What parish are you in, Manny?"

I chuckle and pause. "Father, today was the first time I've gone to Mass in eleven years."

"Welcome back."

"Well, I'm not *back*. Sheila just asked me to join her today, and—"

He cuts me off with a laugh. "And, let me guess, you wanted to be with her so much you couldn't say no," he says.

"You got it, Max." There's something about the directness of this guy that I like.

So ol' Father Max—I mean, young Father Max—changes the subject.

"Manny, I'd love to see you play. Got any concerts coming up?"

I don't see a lot of guys in collars at my shows. "Nothing right now, but this new agent's gonna book some local gigs for us soon." I smile. "All priests will be invited."

Father Max nods as his phone rings. A minute later, he is excusing himself. "Mrs. Rayburn is on her death bed. Got to go and anoint her in the Sacrament of the Sick. All in a day's work. Nice meeting you, Manny. Sheila, always good to see you."

15

♩. ♪ *I love the way you look,*
  I love the way you smile
  You bring bliss to my life,
  I love your style. ♪ 𝆹

"What You Do to Me"
— The Dukes (Manny Morrison)

Over the next couple of months, things get busy. With the prospect of recording on Jupiter Records, me, Billy, and Crash really get after it. We polish the last four songs we need for the CD, and the one and only Wally 'Waldo' Wallace books us at three different venues to test out the new material on stage.

Sheila and Rachel are at each concert, and Father Max shows up at the last one. Quite a sight to see the young collar man groovin' next to Sheila on the dance floor.

Meanwhile, me and Sheila are growing closer. I fully realize that there are a lot of groupies out there, and the number's just gonna grow when the CD comes out, but I can't see myself finding anyone who's such a total package. I mean, Sheila has looks, class, brains, humor—and faith. Well, I could do without the faith part, but I respect her for it. She's a bold, confident woman, and I love that. If you want to know the truth, I love *her.*

So on a picture-perfect Saturday morning in June, I'm having coffee with Sheila and Rachel on the small deck of Sheila's apartment. Rachel is bemoaning her troubles with men.

"All they want is my body. Manny, do you know one single guy who's not going to want to drop his pants on the first date?"

I feel for Rachel. Sometimes beauty can lead to problems. Maybe Rachel needs to think outside the box. "I've got a possibility for you."

"Who?"

"Billy."

I can tell she's surprised. "Billy? Billy, your bass player?"

"That's the guy."

Rachel looks at Sheila. Sheila's thinking. Sheila's always thinking. Love that about her.

"Rachel, how *about* Billy?"

Rachel shrugs and says, "Well, he's no Steve Bronson."

Sheila gets up and starts walking around the deck. "Well, you're right, not in the physique department. But Rachel, that's what you want to avoid right now. Besides, you're doing what you hate for men to do to you. You're judging him by his body. Anyway, Billy's a big-time talent, Rachel. You've seen him play." She turns to me. "Manny, why do you think Billy?"

I take a sip of coffee before I respond. "Well—I'm not saying it would be a match made in heaven, but hey, Billy's a nice guy. He's a dedicated musician. Now, he's had his problems, but I can tell you, Rachel, the big man's got a sensitive side."

Sheila sits back down and looks at her friend. "Rachel, you don't have to marry the guy. Would it hurt you to go out with him?"

I can see Rachel's gears turning. "Well," she pauses, folding her arms. "No, I guess it wouldn't hurt. And I *do* love the way he plays."

So I jump in to move things along. "How about if I give him your number? The band's off next Saturday."

I see Rachel thinking. "Well—okay. At least then I can check one more thing off my bucket list: Go out with a boy in a band."

16

♩♪ Waiting for the flowers,
waiting for the train,
Waiting to see you, nothing to lose,
everything to gain. ♪ 𝅗𝅥·

"Waiting"
— The Dukes (Manny Morrison)

Well, as you can guess, when I give Rachel's number to Billy, he's pretty jazzed and they set something up. But right now, I'm not thinkin' about Billy, I'm thinkin' about Sheila. She's invited me over to dinner and wants to watch a movie. Probably some chick flick, but who cares?

She greets me with a kiss at her door, and takes my hand to lead me inside. I love the silky white blouse she's wearing over her clean jeans. Her hair looks dazzling, and I can't help but think how much time she must have spent shampooing and conditioning and drying and combing and fluffing and spraying, just to look so great for me. My eyes pop when I see her familiar ol' dining room. Except tonight it looks transformed. Her table is covered with a white tablecloth. There are two place settings, complete with cloth napkins and silver I haven't seen before. She's got these tall candles lit in these brass candleholders, and I think, wow, this is gonna be *some* night.

She pours each of us a glass of wine in the kitchen. Can't believe how good it smells in here. No microwave tonight! She pulls this bubbling lasagna out of the oven, and I just want to suck in the aroma. Mmm. She's made a salad with cherry tomatoes and mandarin oranges and artichoke hearts, and I'm more than glad to help her get it to the table.

She adjusts the candles so she can look into my eyes.

"Wow, Sheila. This is great." Her face looks fabulous in the candlelight. "So, um, what's the occasion?"

"Well," she says as I watch the words flow from her lips, "I just thought, you've been working so hard on this CD, and running around here playing these shows, that you might enjoy a nice, quiet night away from the stress."

Boy, do I love a girl who's perceptive. She gets it, even though she hasn't seen the little adjustments to the arrangements, the constant tinkering with the tunes, the hours and hours of practice. I give her a smile.

"This is perfect."

"Manny, I want you to know, I really think you're special." She laughs. "That day we met at Kaldi's, and you were singing that silly song, well, some things were obvious—you could sing, and you were good-looking. But I had no idea who you were, or that someday, we'd be together like this."

I had no idea, either. We've come a long way. "Sheila, you're special to me, too."

Well, we drain the bottle of wine, chow down on Sheila's fantastic feast, and then she says, "Hey, big boy—I've got a surprise for you."

I'm thinkin'—nah, that would be too good to be true. Anyway, she heads to the kitchen and brings out these whipped-cream-covered chocolate mousse parfaits and coffee.

Then she catches me off guard. "Manny—how do you feel about having children?"

I gulp. *Children?* Where is she going here? Well, there's no reason not to tell her how I feel. "I love kids. I mean, I *love* 'em. I always wanted to have brothers and sisters. How 'bout you?"

She takes a deep breath and smiles. "I feel the same. I was an only child, too. I just think it would be *awesome* to be a mother."

Well, Sheila would be about the most beautiful mother in the world, I can see that, but this ain't no time for that kind of commitment. So I tell her, "I'm sure you will be a tremendous mom someday."

She pauses and adjusts the collar of her blouse. "Yeah, but I've got to make sure I'm with the right man before I would ever have a child." Then she looks at me as if to say, "Right now, you're the leading candidate," but before I can respond, she says, "Let's go watch the movie."

She grabs a second bottle of wine, and we head to the couch. Well, no surprise, she's picked this romantic flick, and I can tell she's really into it. Me, not so much. But I've got my arm around her perfect waist, and she's got her head on my shoulder. Nice.

Well, I don't know if she's just feeling mellow, but before too long, she drinks about three-quarters of the bottle of wine. Mercifully, the movie comes to an end, and I start to slowly massage her back. We kiss, and the kissing becomes more and more passionate. I don't know if it's the wine or what, but she seems unusually amorous tonight. I caress her thick, soft hair, and she rubs her fingers through mine. My every breath is filled with the intoxicating aroma of her perfume.

I adjust my position and gently caress her neck. Softly, I trace her cheeks and her chin, and gaze deeply into those crystal clear blue eyes. I exhale, then I breathe in and smile as I move next to her and wrap my arms around her in a tender embrace.

I'm half expecting her to say something like, "Let's be careful now" or "watch yourself." But to my surprise, she welcomes my lips, and we kiss even more passionately than before. I'm beginning to think, wow, this could be it. This could be the night—.

BAM-BAM-BAM-BAM-BAM. What the—who the hell is pounding on the door?

"Sheila! Sheila!" a frantic female voice shrieks. Whoever it is, she sounds hysterical. The beating on the door grows louder. Sheila pulls away from me and runs toward the pounding. The second she unbolts the lock, the door flies open.

It's Rachel!

The always perfectly groomed Rachel looks worse than I've ever seen her. Her blonde hair is a mess. Mascara is running down her cheeks. Her blouse is untucked in the back. She falls on the couch, and Sheila rushes to her side.

"Rachel, are you alright? What the hell happened?"

Rachel groans and exhales. "It was Billy. I thought he was going to rape me."

I'm stunned. *Rape?* What is she talking about?

Rachel looks almost too shaken up to speak. She cups her face with her hands, and shakes her head as she sobs.

Sheila has her arm around her. "Rachel, try to relax. Take your time. Now, tell me what happened."

It takes a while, but Rachel's breathing begins to slow down. "Billy and I went out to dinner. Nothing fancy. We were at Applebee's. So everything's fine. He's a little nervous. He told me he hasn't been out with anybody for a while. So we chat. I told him how much I love the band. Told him I think he's great. Well, after we eat, he asks me if I'd like to see his posters and guitars.

"So I'm thinking, 'why not?' We get to his apartment, and he starts showing me his stuff, and then says, 'I've got to go to the bathroom.' Well, he's in there for a long time, and when he comes back out, he has totally changed. His eyes are glazed over and bloodshot. Right away, I say, 'Billy, I've got to go.' But he's not having it. He wraps his arms around my waist and tries to kiss me. I try to push him away, but he's too strong. He tries to kiss me again, and I scream. He lets go, and I run out the door."

So I say, "So—he really didn't try to rape you?"

Well, Rachel just bursts into tears and sobs into Sheila's shoulder. Sheila glares at me, and says, "Manny! I think you better get out of here."

So I slink out of there, and seek refuge in the Camaro. I'm sitting behind Sheila's apartment complex, too stunned to turn the key. I pound on the steering wheel. My head's about to explode.

This is too hard to believe. I might have been 10 minutes away from ecstasy with the most beautiful woman I've ever known, and then everything falls apart.

What the hell is Billy doing? Damn those drugs! I thought he was finally done with this.

I grab my phone. The second Billy answers, I yell, "What the hell is wrong with you?"

Billy slurs, "What are ya talkin' about, man?"

"You kidding me?" I'm shouting now. "Why would you do that to Rachel? Since when are you back on drugs? Do you care about the band? Do you care about yourself? Do you care about *anything?*"

He mutters, "I'm not back on drugs." Yeah, right. It's not worth talking to him right now. I can't hang up fast enough.

17

~ *Sheila* ~

My head is spinning after the last ten hours. It took near-ly all night to calm Rachel down. I can't believe Billy did that to her. And I can't believe Manny said that! And I can't believe how close *I* got. I mean, what would have happened if Rachel hadn't shown up when she did? I mean, I really, really, really like Manny—but is it worth it? I feel like my priorities are all out of whack lately.

I know what I need to do.

"Lord, thank You for protecting Rachel last night. Bil-ly could have overpowered her. That would have been a tragedy. But what about me, Lord? Rachel was inno-cent, but I wasn't. I was about to give Manny all I've got. What was I thinking? How did I get there? Three months of dating a musician? Was that all it took to give up what You've wanted me to save for my future husband?

"Lord, is Manny my future husband? Can You let me know? I've never been so attracted to anyone. It's not just his looks and his talent, Lord, it's his heart. You gave him a great heart. I almost melted when he said he loves kids.

"You know he's had a tough life. Losing his mom at 14? I can understand why he blames You for that. And what about his dad? I can't imagine getting a phone call in the middle of the night that my dad died thousands of miles away. So his parents weren't there for him. And then he meets Steve. All Steve thinks about is sex. Some example, Lord! How can I prove to Manny that sex is a fabulous, beautiful gift reserved for marriage with Steve telling him the direct opposite all the time? Of course, that would be blaming Steve for something I almost did.

"Lord, I need your help. Please, Lord! How can I show Manny that sex isn't everything?

"Terrell? What? Why am I suddenly thinking about Terrell? Oh, wait. Terrell…of course! Oh, wow, Lord! That's it! Terrell! Terrell! Thank You, Lord! When Manny meets Terrell, he's going to see what life is all about."

18

Shooting, snorting,
smooking—he's addicted,
He's all messed up, he's conflicted,
Will he ever return?

"The Road to Where?"
— The Dukes (Manny Morrison)

The first thing I'm going to do the next morning is call Billy, but he beats me to it.

"Hey, Manny, I just want to tell you, I'm really sorry about last night. I don't know what came over me."

Well, for a couple of minutes, I just go off on him.

"Sorry? Sorry's not gonna cut it, Billy. If you had gone any further with Rachel, I'd be talking to you in jail. You've been clean for months. I thought you were done with that shit. And what about the band? Do you know how close we are? Do you even care?"

Billy shouts back. "You know I care! I care just as much as you do, Manny."

"Then why the hell did you go back to that shit?"

"Manny, I didn't want to, it's just, I was so nervous.

I've never been out with a woman like Rachel."

I try to keep my composure. "Billy, you can't run back to that stuff every time a girl makes you nervous. You need help, man."

He grunts. "Listen, I've been through all that. Rehab doesn't work for me."

"Have you been goin' to N.A.?"

Billy sighs. "Well, I was going for the first six months but I really didn't get along with those guys. And I was doing so well, I thought it was no big deal."

I'm disappointed to hear this. "Listen man, you gotta get help. I'm not gonna watch you slip back down this path."

"Manny, it was one time! I'm fine. It's not gonna happen again."

"Billy, I don't want to hear it. Rehab doesn't work? Okay, fine. But you need *something*.

I pound a fist into my hand and then, out of nowhere, an idea hits me. "Billy, I want to help you, man. Get your butt over here at 2 o'clock this afternoon."

───────── ♪ o 𝄽 ─────────

I'm counting on Lenny to come through. When he played with my dad's band, I'm guessing his habit was as bad as Billy's ever was. I'm takin' a chance here, but it's gonna be bass player to bass player, and maybe it'll work. Lenny's sitting on the red leather couch, wearing his usual 20-year-old jeans. His long hair touches the top of his T-shirt from the concert he played last night in Kansas

City. He was born the same year as my dad, so he's a couple of decades older than Billy and me. Me and Lenny don't talk much about our personal lives, so he was surprised when I asked him to talk to Billy. He knows him from a couple of jam sessions we've had, but since Lenny spends 250 nights a year on the road, there hasn't been much time to jam.

I'm relieved when Billy shows up, but I know from the look on his face, he has no idea why I asked him to come over.

Billy fills the recliner in the corner of the room. "Hey, Lenny."

Well, Lenny just jumps in like a fighter roaring out of the corner at the opening bell. "Listen, Billy, I'm not here to bullshit you. I know where you've been, and I'm not just talking about last night. I've been there, too, and then some. Kid, I was on drugs almost longer than you've been alive, and I thought I'd never quit. But one night changed all that. You probably heard somethin' about it."

Billy looks at me. "Was that the night your dad—"

Lenny cuts him off. "Listen! Duke Morrison and I played together since we were five years old. Yeah, we never became the Rolling Stones, but we made a lot more dough than most people, and we had a helluva time doing it. It was mostly because of Duke. The guy was something else.

"Well, it didn't seem any different that night in Fresno. We knocked out the crowd and went back to the hotel. We had scored all kinds of shit earlier that day. We'd been partying for hours. So when Duke hit the floor, I thought he just passed out. Wouldn't have been the first time. But after a while, when I checked him, Duke wasn't breathing. I pounded on his chest, tried every way I could to revive him. But he was gone. For good."

Lenny leans forward until his butt's almost off the couch. He stares at Billy. He slowly growls out every word. "Do you know what it's like to sit next to your dead best friend?"

Billy looks like he can hardly breathe.

Lenny leans in again. "Can you imagine what it's like to watch your best friend die—and you don't even know it?"

Lenny sits back on the couch and takes a deep breath. "I vowed that night that I'd never touch the stuff again. And to this day, I haven't."

I've heard the story many times, but Billy never has. Not like this. His eyes grow wide. Nobody says nothin' for quite a while. Billy looks at me, then back at Lenny.

"Lenny, it's not like I want to do this. It's not like I want to die. And despite last night, I've been doing really good. But the call is always there. After what you've shared, I know *why* you stay away, but what do you do when, you know, it's right there in front of you?"

Well, right now, I'm thinkin', maybe it's best for these two guys who've been in the same place to talk this out alone. So I stand up and say, "Guys, I think I'm gonna go for a little walk."

To my surprise, Lenny says, "No, Manny. I think it would be good for you to hear this, too."

125

So I sit back down. Wonder why he wants me here. Lenny stares at Billy. "Listen. You got to find something that's more important to you than a high. Something that's more real. And I found it."

"What'd you find?"

"I found Jesus Christ."

Billy lets out a low groan. I'm surprised beyond words.

"No, Billy, I'm not about to preach to you. You asked what I found, so here it is. It's Jesus Christ, but in a way I never knew Him before. It's Jesus, disguised as a small piece of bread."

I can't keep my jaw from dropping. I've *never* heard Lenny talk about this.

"You see, when Duke died, I didn't know what I was gonna do. My best friend was gone, and so was the band. Well, they had the funeral at the Catholic church back home, even though Duke never went to church anywhere. But it made sense that he'd be buried by the same church as his wife, Manny's mother, and laid to rest next to her.

"At the gravesite, after everyone else had left, even you, Manny, I was standing there alone with the priest. I told him, 'Father, I don't know how I can go on.' And he looks at me and says, 'Oh, you can, son.' I'll never forget the kindness in his eyes. Then he says, 'Come by and see me at the rectory tomorrow morning.'

"I had been raised Catholic, but I hadn't been to church since I was a kid. Still, I didn't know where else to go, so I went and saw the priest. I leveled with him. I told him I was thinking about suicide. He says—and I'll never forget this—'My son, life is a gift.' I had never thought about it like that. I thought that I just *had* life. And then he says, 'Jesus gave up His life as a gift for us. And He did so much more. In fact, when He ascended into heaven, He wanted to remain here with us, and He's here with us today.'"

Lenny smiles. "So I looked around the priest's office, and I didn't see anybody."

Billy chuckles.

"Well, the priest gets up and leads me into a little chapel, adjacent to the church. There's this gold container on the altar with the host inside. The priest kneels on one side of the little chapel, and I kneel on the other. He makes the sign of the cross, and I just stare at the host.

"It's very hard to describe this, and it may be hard for you to believe, but in that instant, I somehow knew that the host was Jesus Christ, present, right then and there. So I say to the Lord, 'I'm helpless. I need You. Please help me.' The night Duke died I vowed to never do drugs again, but here in this chapel, I found the *strength* I needed to help me keep that promise."

Billy looks stunned. I am *more* than stunned.

Lenny looks at Billy. "Man, I play 250 gigs a year. I've played hundreds and hundreds since Duke died. But wherever we play, whatever city we're in, I find a Catholic church, and I kneel before the King of Kings. And in Him I find peace. And it's Him that's kept me clean these past three years."

I slump back on the couch. I'm blown away. I mean, I

have no idea what Lenny does when he's on the road, but going to chapels wasn't even on my radar. Billy slowly stands up. All the color is drained from his face. He looks like he just got punched in the gut. He looks at Lenny and says, "You've given me a lot to think about." He lets out a long, low breath. "Thanks. Really."

I'm still trying to process. I turn to Lenny. "Is all that true?"

He looks me in the eye, and slowly speaks. "Every word."

I don't know what to say. "Why haven't you ever told me?"

"I didn't think you were in a place to hear it." Lenny chuckles. "You never know when someone's going to open their ears."

Billy heads for the door. Lenny stops him.

"Billy?"

"Yeah?"

"You're about to record on *Jupiter Records!*" Lenny points a finger at Billy's chest. *"Don't screw this up!"*

19

*♩.♪ School's out, getting hot,
  music playing loud,
  T-shirts, cutoffs, runnin' with the crowd,
  Ah, sweet summertime. ♪ ○·*

"Summer"
— Manny Morrison (age 16)

The next day, me and Steve are having lunch in the Members' Grille at the Country Club of St. Louis. Steve's deal with the Rams includes the club membership. And that's in addition to the 66.6 million bucks. He's got a hell of an agent.

So I bring him up to date on our progress toward the upcoming recording session at Jupiter Records and praise the work of my manager, Wally 'Waldo' Wallace. By the way, Mr. Six loves the guy's nickname. We clink our scotch glasses in tribute to our agents.

Before long, as usual, Steve turns the conversation to his favorite subject: women.

"How's that brunette, what's her name?" He's teasing me now.

"*Sheila's* great."

"So, have you guys finally—you know?"

"Well, not 'all the way.'" Actually, I haven't even gotten to second base, but I'm not gonna tell him that.

"Huh?" Steve looks at me with disbelief. "What do you mean?"

I smile. "I think she was close to deciding to do it this weekend, but, uh—"

I pause. What am I gonna tell him? *You know that girl you used to date, Steve? The one you dumped because she wouldn't sleep with you? Can you believe she almost got date raped? By your friend and mine, Billy the Bass Player?*

"—uh, something came up, and we got interrupted. But, we'll get there. Definitely."

Steve shakes his head. "Well, good. I mean, how long are you gonna wait?"

"No worries, Steve. It'll be in your lifetime."

Steve smiles. "Great." He finally moves on. "Hey, by the way, you know training camp's about to start, which means I'm gonna be locked away with about 90 football animals for about the next three weeks, so for a while, you'll only be seeing me on TV." Steve seems relaxed and confident. He finishes his scotch. "You know, Manny, you're a great friend. You've been there for me since my first week here. So I got you a little gift—a pair of prime season tickets—50 yard line."

Wow, I didn't expect this. "Steve, thanks so much. Man, that's great!" I pause. "A pair, huh? You know, I don't even know if Sheila likes football."

Steve grins. "You think come September, you're still gonna be dating Sheila?"

I down the rest of my scotch. "Oh, yeah. I'm *sure* I'm still gonna be dating Sheila."

The next Saturday morning, Sheila calls and says she'd like me to come over and meet somebody. But she won't say who. Well, on the way over I'm wondering who the hell it could be. Does she have a new boyfriend? Nah. But that *would* be a disaster! Maybe she picked up a pet.

Anyway, when I walk into her apartment, she gives me a quick little hug and says, "Manny, I'd like you to meet Terrell." And before I can say anything, I am bull-rushed by this short, stocky man-in-motion. In a blur, he runs up to me and wraps his arms around me and gives me a hug that almost stops my breathing. I'm looking down at the top of his head—he must be about 5'3"—and I'm wondering if he's ever gonna let go. When I'm just about to expire, he breaks his arms apart, takes a step back, and gives me the biggest smile I've ever seen.

"Hi, Manny! I'm Terrell Washington!" he cackles. Now, I never use the word "cackles," but that's the best way I can describe it. I'm sure I've never met anyone so filled with joy just to meet me.

"Uh—hi, Terrell!"

I glance at Sheila. She's got this coy smile on her lips. "Remember in Chicago, when you asked me about the 'craziest thing' ever, and I told you about the guy who—?"

Suddenly it clicks. Ah, Terrell! It's coming back now. This must be her client, the one who did the handstand—and accidentally kicked the guy in the face.

"Oh, yeah, I remember."

Sheila is glowing. "Well, this is the one and only Terrell. He lives in a group home. He doesn't get out much, so I volunteer to pick him up one Saturday a month."

Terrell nods his head with such vigor I'm afraid he may hurt himself. He thrusts his hand into the air and I give him a high-five. Instant connection. I look over to Sheila and tell her, "You're terrific."

She responds with a shake of her head. "You know, back in the 17th century, the great St. Vincent de Paul said we can't just *serve* the poor, we should be *friends* to the poor. Terrell and I are friends."

Terrell is beaming. "Yep. And Manny, you can be our friend, too!" I answer with a smile, and another high-five. He doesn't slow down. "I'm hungry. Manny, you hungry?"

"Well, sure, Terrell, I could eat."

He's almost giddy. "We're going to Burger King, right, Sheila? Burger King, Burger King, Burger King!"

She grins. "Hope you don't feel rushed, but Terrell doesn't like to sit around."

"Got that."

"Burger King's his favorite restaurant."

"Got that, too."

In the car, Terrell talks nonstop. "Sheila told me you're

a musician, Manny. I love music."

"Yeah? What kind of music do you like?"

Terrell thinks for a half-second. "Rap, hip-hop, rock, country."

"Whoa, you're all over the place."

"Yeah, I listen to music all day long."

Sheila gives me a look filled with compassion. "There's not much else he's allowed to do in the group home."

Suddenly, Terrell starts ticking off the names and titles of his favorite songs and artists, and sure enough, he's covering about four different genres. I'm amazed. You ever see the movie, "Rain Man?" Well, Terrell's like the Rain Man of music.

When we get to Burger King, each food line is about four people deep. Not pleasing to Terrell. "Sheila, I don't want to wait in line. Get me a Whopper with fries and a Coke, okay?" Sheila grins, as if this has happened before. "Same for me," I smile, reaching into my pocket for some money. She waves off the dough and gets in line.

Terrell slaps me on the back and says, "Let's go over here, Manny." So we walk over to an empty space in the lobby of the King.

"Guess what, Manny?"

"What?"

"I can do the splits." Uh-oh. Sheila's story about the handstand incident pops into my head.

"I, um, uh—I bet you can."

He starts nodding as if there's no doubt. "Manny, can you do the splits?"

I let out a nervous little laugh. "Well, um, I—"

In the next instant, Terrell claps his hands, then his feet slide apart, his legs and butt touch the ground, and he pops back up. It's like—the perfect splits. I'm stunned. Amazing. "Whoa, Terrell! Wow!"

He bursts into a smile and says, "That's what I do sometimes when I'm listening to music." Then he pauses. "Can you do that?"

Whew. This is an awkward moment. I look over his head at the people standing in line, and then I glance out the window. Then, all of a sudden, I whip my boots sideways, hit the ground, pop back up, and finish with a 360-degree spin.

Terrell explodes with joy. He whoops and claps his hands. "Manny can do the splits!" he announces to the entire restaurant. And his voice keeps getting louder. "Manny can *really* do the splits." Well, heads turn, and just in case anyone guesses that I'm *Manny,* I just shrug as if I don't know what he's talking about.

Terrell rushes to me and delivers another near back-breaking hug. "You're *great,* Manny! You're great!" And I'm thinking the same thing about him.

Sheila brings over the food, we eat, and then we drop Terrell off at the group home. He's sad when we have to part, and so are we.

Back at Sheila's apartment, I say, "I think it's terrific that you get him out of there once a month. Terrell's so *full of life."*

"No question about that. You know, we're all supposed to see Christ in others, and it's easy to see Him in Terrell."

"Yep. I guess." *Why is she bringing Christ into this?*

I give her a quick hug and tell her I've got to run, and that I'm really looking forward to coming back to see her later that night. "It's *so* unfortunate we were interrupted last week."

"Uh, Manny, I've got something to tell you. Let's sit down for a minute."

So I'm wondering what this is all about, and—

"Manny, I was almost thinking of giving in last weekend, and I just want to let you know that I don't want us to go *there* again."

I'm surprised. Well, more than *surprised.* "What do you mean?"

"I mean, I could have lost my virginity last week, and once you lose it, you can never get it back. Manny, I really, really like you, and—I'll go ahead and say it—I *love* you. But I'm going to save myself for my husband."

Can't believe this. I'm stunned. *Truly* stunned. Hell, I thought we were on the way just last Saturday. Maybe I'm wrong, but I think we were *going in that direction,* and if it hadn't been for Rachel and Billy—and now this?

"Manny, I've been wanting to introduce you to Terrell, and I especially wanted you to meet him today. You can see how easy it is to see the Lord in him. Well, I can see the Lord so easily in you, too. But the Lord wants us to love and serve Him in each other, not *use* each other."

I'm speechless.

Then she leans forward, and I can sense her emotions welling up. Her voice breaks down into a near whisper. "Manny, if I ever marry you, I will give you all I've got. All of me, and with great passion and joy, and again and again and again. I know it'll be fantastic. But until then, we've got to wait."

20

♩.♪ Don't know what's goin' on tomorrow,
Hardly know what's goin' on today. ♪ o·

"Mystery"
— The Dukes (Manny Morrison)

Shit. I'm back at my place. I just don't get it. She said she loved me. Even mentioned the 'M' word. And if this is how she really feels, well, what about last week? Damn it! She was softening up, I know it, I could feel it. So, what's changed?

The funny thing about her is, she can make me feel so great, and then in one second, I'm totally frustrated. Like Steve says, how long can a guy hold out? Steve would say to dump her, but I can't do that. Sheila's not just some "flavor of the week."

It was so *great* to hear her say that she loves me. I *knew* that she does, and I love her, too, but to hear her say those words, well—I've never had any woman say that to me and mean it like she does. She's special. You know, who else would give up part of a Saturday every month to bring some joy into the life of Terrell? I remember how my mom used to say, there are two kinds of people in this world—givers and takers. Well, Sheila's definitely a giver. But why won't she give herself to me?

And yet, she *does* give herself to me—kinda. I mean, even when she takes me to church, I think that she's trying to do me some good. And I don't know who she thought she was helping more today, me or Terrell, but it was somethin' else being with that little man. Terrell's a joy-spreading machine! I could see him accidentally kicking a guy in the face in his *exuberance.* With Terrell, there's no holding back. With Sheila, it's *all* holding back. Damn.

What am I going to do? I pick up a guitar, one that my dad gave me just before he died. I start wandering around, strumming away, going through some of our new songs. Eventually, I play the one I like best. The one I know is gonna be big, and in the midst of everything, it brings me joy. And for some reason, Terrell pops into my head. And I can't hold back. At the end of the song, I do the splits. And I finish with a 360-degree spin.

Two hours later, Wally 'Waldo' Wallace is on the phone.

"Manny, things are right on schedule. You'll be recording at Jupiter no later than this fall. In the meantime, got a nice gig for you and The Dukes. It's in Omaha."

I'm underwhelmed. *Omaha?*

"Here's the reason for this—we want to start your expansion around the Midwest. I'm setting you up at a place called "The Waiting Room." Nobody's going to know you in Omaha. But by the end of the night, I'm betting they're *all* going to remember you."

Guess that kinda makes sense. "This is a paid gig, right?"

"Manny, Manny, Manny. You're not dealing with Sonny Jenkins anymore. It's $5,000, and you and the guys can split it any way you want. I've got the hotel and the plane covered. You can even take your girlfriend."

I think about that. Gotta believe Waldo knows what he's doing. "All right. Sounds good. When is it?"

"Two weeks from Friday. I'll email you the details."

"Okay. And, uh—thanks, Waldo."

"Trust me, Manny. I know what I'm doing."

When I was hoping to sleep with Sheila this evening, I made plans to take her to a nice dinner at Frazier's. Even though she let me know there's gonna be *no action*, I take her to Frazier's anyway. That's just the kind of 'classy' guy I am.

During dinner, we talk about everything. Even church.

"Did you know that Lenny visits a church in every city when he's on the road?"

A look of surprise appears on her face. "No. Lenny? He does?"

I nod. "Yep."

She folds her arms. "Why didn't you tell me that before?"

"I just found out last week, when Lenny was trying to help Billy. He was tellin' him, 'you need something stronger than drugs.' He sure surprised me."

139

She looks thoughtful. "Well, that's great, Manny! I'm sure it helps him with all the temptations on the road."

Speaking of temptations on the road, I really want Sheila to go to Omaha with me. It's just good to have her at my concerts. I don't know what she's gonna say, but when I ask her she says, 'Yes!' And I'm feeling *really* good about that. Except for one thing.

"Manny, I'm sure you can guess—we won't be sleeping together."

21

♩· ♪ *We're gonna wail and*
womp and stick it to you,
We're gonna pound and bring it,
the whole night through ♪ 𝅗𝅥·

"The Wailin' Song"
— The Dukes (Crash)

We get to Omaha in the morning. We're gonna set up two hours before show time tonight, so we have time to kill. Or, time to get nervous. Musicians handle nerves in different ways. For Billy, it's eating. I'm hoping there's still food left in Omaha after we leave. As for Crash, I never know what he's up to. Big-time loner. All I know is—any time, every time, he shows up on time, and beats the hell out of those drums.

For me, I can't stand to sit around. Gotta get out, gotta move. I'm so glad Sheila's with me. We find that our Best Western hotel is less than a mile from Creighton University, so we decide to walk to the school. And wouldn't you know it, right there, smack dab in the middle of campus, there's this gigantic, old Catholic church.

Naturally, Sheila wants to go inside. It doesn't take long before she's on her knees in front of the tabernacle. I decide it's not gonna kill me to kneel next to her—at least for a couple of minutes. Man, it's hard to imagine Lenny doing this when he's on the road! When did all these people get religion?

Sheila closes her eyes, so I close mine. Monkey see, monkey do. I figure she's praying, so I say—silently of course—"Jesus, don't know if You're in there, but Sheila sure thinks You are. I know she really loves You. And she told me she loves me, too. I'm wonderin' where we're headed. I think the *band's* goin' forward. Oh, by the way, if that was You up there in Chicago—thanks. It went great. And, uh, we got another gig tonight. Would it be greedy if I asked You to do somethin' special for us? At least help my man, Billy, realize what we got going here, so, uh, please keep him clean. And please help me and Sheila. And, uh, amen."

I open my eyes. To my surprise, Sheila's sitting down. So I get off my knees and sit next to her. She leans over and whispers, "I just want to sit and listen to the Lord."

Okay. Well, a minute goes by. "I don't hear anything."

She looks at me and laughs, and says, "Just one more minute." So I lean back and marvel at the structure of this place—it must be over a hundred years old—and my eyes are drawn to the crucifix. Still don't know what to make of *that.*

Anyway, Sheila makes the sign of the cross, and we're out of there. Whew. Another city, another church.

I'm getting to be like Lenny.

♪ o ♭

Music ain't all glamour. I've played in some real dives. A few of them, you wouldn't believe, but I won't go into that. Luckily, "The Waiting Room" is cool. They tell me they do shows here five and six days a week, and I can tell it's a savvy music crowd that shows up on this Friday night. Two bands are playing, and we're first up. The good thing is, we get to play for an hour in front of a crowd that's never seen us. A chance to prove ourselves. Thank you, Waldo.

To be honest, when we hit the stage, the crowd is not exactly going crazy. That's okay. We're from out of town. They've never heard our songs. But when Crash picks up his sticks and starts banging, and big Billy begins dropping the bass line, and I get to strumming, the mood changes in a hurry. Like I told you, I know when we're sounding good, and we're super tight tonight. We've pretty much won the crowd over by the end of the first song, and from there, it keeps getting better.

Can't say if it's Waldo coming up with the booking, or the anticipation of recording at Jupiter, or the fact that we're actually making some decent bucks or what, but this is the best we've ever played. And to make it sweeter, Sheila's there, swaying and dancing in the front row. Her face radiates joy. All is well with the world.

We save our best song for last. Wanna finish big. Well, halfway through it, this crowd, a crowd that's never heard the song before, is really rockin'! The place is electric!

And I'm feeling that musician's high in every fiber of my body, a natural high that's impossible to explain. This is what I live for.

So as we rock into the last chorus, I'm all but overcome with joy. And for some reason, the joy of Terrell pops into my head. That uninhibited, free spirited joy, the joy of feeling so alive. For a second, I'm with Terrell back at Burger King. I can't hold back. As I sing and play the last line of the song, I do the splits!

Well, the crowd roars! Billy and Crash are feeling it, so we instinctively repeat the last line. And I do the splits again, while I'm strumming. What happens seems incredible. The roar increases. So we hit' em with the last line again. For a third time, I drop down and do the splits. This time I use a windmill strum, and then I pop up to finish with a 360-degree spin. The crowd goes crazy!

I can't resist taking off my guitar, holding it high to the crowd, and giving them a heartfelt, full-throated "Thank you!" They're *roaring* as we exit the stage.

———————— ♪ o ♭ ————————

Gotta celebrate. Me and Sheila and Billy and Crash head down the street to a bar and order drinks. Sheila whips out her phone and says, "Look at this!" She plays the video of our last song. I didn't even see her recording it. Anyway, we see the finale, and we all crack up.

"Sheila, you gotta send me that!" I immediately tweet it to Steve. It'll give him something to laugh about before he heads to training camp.

Billy chugs a beer. He's beside himself. "What got into you, man? Where the hell did you get that move?"

If he had only been there with us at Burger King— "You wouldn't believe me if I told you."

"Manny, from my spot on the stage, I thought you fell down." Billy's having fun. "I was gonna help you up. But *clearly,* you didn't need any help."

Crash, being Crash, drawls, "I thought you were drunk, man." So as we continue to laugh our asses off, Steve tweets back, "My favorite tweet of the year. You're a wild man!"

"Steve just called me a wild man."

"Huh?"

"I just tweeted him the video."

Sheila laughs and tweets it to Rachel.

"Here's her response. 'You got a flexible boyfriend there, honey! Where'd he get that move?'"

I'm thinkin' this is definitely the most fun we could ever have in Omaha.

22

♩.♪ *Things lookin' up, rocket to the moon,*
Where's it all goin',
gonna find out soon. ♪ o·

"Moving"
— The Dukes (Manny Morrison)

It's always fun to share videos with friends, so I thought there was a chance we'd get a few more hoots out of the video from "The Waiting Room." I didn't expect a *viral explosion.*

Here's what happens. Steve tweets it as "must see," and he's got 1.1 million followers. Including many other studs in the NFL. Well, you know how retweets go. Then, Waldo starts to push it on social media. Suddenly, my triple-splits-with-360 is *all over* the internet. YouTube explodes. It gets 23 million hits in a week. 50,000 new people view it every *hour.*

My head's spinning. I'm sitting on the wrap-around when my phone rings. "Manny, you got to be glad you've got me to manage this chaos."

"Hey, you're right about that, Waldo."

I hear him laugh. "You're the only guy who calls me Waldo, but I'm gonna let that go. Just callin' to tell you, we're gonna record at Jupiter Records in three weeks."

I'm shocked. "Three *weeks?* I thought it was gonna be more like three months."

"Things change in this biz. When we're hot, we gotta move fast."

Whoa. "Man, we were gearing up to record this fall. I don't know if we can be ready."

Waldo doesn't hesitate. "You gotta be, Manny. YouTube fame has a short lifespan. And while we're talking, I got another thing for you, and this is great, and yes, you're gonna be ready. Since millions of people suddenly want to see you do the splits, I've got you booked as one of three acts at this huge show a week from Wednesday. TD Garden. Boston."

My head is spinning. Boston! My old college town. Only this time, I won't be playing the dive bars around the Fens. I'll be jammin' at the home of the Celtics! The home of the Bruins! "Boston beats Omaha, my man."

Waldo immediately replies, "Hey, listen to me, and listen good. *Never* dis Omaha, pal. Never for the rest of your life. You hear me? We'll talk tomorrow."

I exhale and plop down on the couch. This is almost overwhelming. I mean, it's all great, but this is also a lot of pressure. Gotta call Billy and Crash. Gotta keep their heads on straight. Gotta keep 'em focused. Gotta set up rehearsals.

But I call Sheila first.

I give her the news about Boston. I ask her to go with me, but she says she has to work. My heart sinks.

"Why don't you take two or three vacation days?"

"Manny—poverty doesn't take a vacation."

Well, I see her point, but it's going to be a lot harder to do this without her. She always calms me down. I let it all soak in. Instead of being with me in Beantown, she's gonna be at St. Vincent de Paul, serving those in need. This chick is truly one-of-a-kind.

"Manny, the way things are going, there's going to be plenty more big shows."

"I know. But who's going to shoot the video in Boston?"

She laughs. "Oh, I'm sure you'll have a million groupies volunteering."

23

Boston, Boston, beans and Paul Revere,
Books and Back Bay, gonna love it here

"Beantown"
— Manny Morrison (age 18)

Of all the cities in the country, Boston is my favorite. Soon after we arrive, I walk the campus at Berklee. Can't help but think of my old man. He was so proud of me for studying at such a great music school. He grew up playing by ear, and I learned from him. But he also wanted me to have the formal training he never had.

Man, I wish he could see me now. I don't know, maybe he can. He might be up there, sitting on a cloud. If so, I bet he's strumming his guitar. Thinking of Dad makes me think of Mom. She's probably up there praying for me. Seems like she was *always* praying for me.

Anyway, I head down to the Public Garden. And this is one of the things I love about Boston. What other bustling city has a place of beauty like this, right in the middle of downtown? It's my very favorite place on earth. I used to come here to relax before exams. Love the flowers, the willow trees, the swan boats, the walking bridge in the middle of the park.

Got a few hours before I have to meet Billy and Crash to get ready. I sit down on a park bench. In the midst of all the chaos, I just want to breathe for a while. So I'm listening to the chirping of the birds when I hear someone yell.

"Manny! Manny, good to see ya!"

I look up and see the overalls.

"Oscar! What the hell are you—"

"Manny, I just *had* to be here for the show tonight! So sorry I missed you in Omaha. Every device I have is exploding with your video. It's crazy, man!"

"Oscar, I think you're my most loyal fan." I catch myself saying, "It's good to see you."

Oscar beams and sits himself down next to me on the bench. "What are you doing here, Manny? I thought you'd be staying down by the arena."

"It's a good place to relax. I'm kinda nervous about the show. Wanted Sheila to come with me, but she had to work. Don't you have to work?"

"My boss knows I'm here." He grins. "And what's there to be nervous about? When you do that splits thing tonight, everyone's gonna go wild."

"Yeah, maybe. But there's a lot of things that could go wrong."

"Like what?"

"Well—I could break a string. Billy could faint. Crash could knock over the drums. The power could go out. The stage could collapse. The building might burn down."

Oscar holds up his hands. "Whoa, whoa, whoa. You're a little uptight here. Man, you gotta calm down." He pauses. "Say, why don't we pray?"

"Pray? About what?"

Oscar laughs. "Listen, Manny, I pray about everything." His eyes move around the park. "Hey, look at that miracle over there."

I follow his gaze. "Where?"

"There."

"Behind the tree?"

"No. The *tree.*"

"That's a tree, not a miracle."

"Ah-ha. Is it? Do you know anyone who can *create* that tree?" He pauses. Tough question. He continues, "Do you know *anyone* who can fashion that trunk, finish that bark, extend those limbs, craft those leaves? Anyone who can make the leaves change color in the fall, drop off in the winter, and grow back in the spring?" He scratches his head. "Do you know *anyone* who can make this tree to withstand the heat and the cold and the Boston wind—for more than 150 years? Manny, I'm sorry, but you're looking at a miracle."

I have no idea what to say. Oscar goes on.

"And look, there's another one next to it. And another. And another. Why, we can't even *count* all the miracles right here in this one park."

I'm thinkin' this guy's loony. What's he talking about?

Oscar stands up and gestures in front of me. "And that's

just the miracle of the trees. How many flowers do you see around here?"

"I don't know. Hundreds."

He chuckles, like I'm way off. "I think if we counted, you might say thousands, maybe hundreds of thousands. All the white ones and the red ones and the pink ones and the purple ones—and all the different varieties."

Still sounds crazy, but I'm thinkin'—no one colored 'em all with *crayons*.

"And Manny, who do you think made this little lake?"

I gaze at the space where the famous swan boats are paddled in the spring and summer. It's only two or three feet deep. "Well, hey, that's clearly a *man-made* lake. There's cement at the bottom."

"No. I'm talking about the *water*."

Again, I don't know what to say.

Oscar smiles. "I'm thinking it might just be the same One who made *all* the water in the oceans and the seas. And everything else, for that matter."

I shake my head. "That's great, Oscar. Pretty cool. Got it. But I gotta play a big concert in a few hours."

"Right. And that's something we can pray for."

Thinkin' of prayer, I'm trying to remember what I said in that chapel in Chicago, and how things went so well. And then in Omaha, how I was kneeling next to Sheila, and I asked for something special, and—holy shit!

"Okay, Oscar, let's pray."

"Great!" He sits down on the park bench across from me. "You know, Manny, you don't have to open your mouth to pray. Why don't you pray in silence, and I'll pray in silence. Right here, right now. Pray from the heart."

So I close my eyes. I pray for Billy and Crash. And I pray that the building won't burn down. I'm about to say, "Amen," but then I think of Sheila. And I pray for her, too.

For the first time all day, I'm feeling at peace. I open my eyes and look up to thank Oscar, but nobody's around.

Strange. I head back to the hotel to get ready for the show. Wonder what Billy and Crash would say if I told them I saw a couple thousand miracles today.

—————— ♪ o ♭ ——————

When we take the stage at TD Garden, I'm thinkin', this won't be much different than Chicago. Boy, am I wrong. Sure, once again, we're the opening act, but this time, we're one of three, not one of 15. In Chicago, it was 11 in the morning, and folks were just strolling in. Here, half the expected crowd of 20,000 are in their seats. And the biggest difference is, the fans recognize us. Power of the internet. Video of my magic move is up to 94 million YouTube hits.

When the lights go down, our adrenaline is flowing. We belt out the first song, and we're tight. The only thing I wish I could change is to see Sheila in the front row. But she's 1,800 miles away. The women I see in her place are dressed in a variety of cleavage-revealing, skin exposing concert wear. Gotta concentrate here, Manny.

We whip through our first eight songs as planned. The

crowd's responsive, but not electric. That changes when I hit the first chords of our biggest song—the one that's rocked the internet—and we hear the roar. I'm lovin' it. Well, as we approach the end of the tune, I know what they came to see, and I'm ready to deliver.

I do the strum and the splits. Big cheer. The strum and the splits again. Now they're *roaring*. One more time, and I finish with the 360-degree spin. They're going *crazy!* They don't stop as we leave the stage. My ears are ringing.

The first person we see behind the curtain is Wally. Good old Waldo. Never seen him so happy. He almost knocks me over as he slaps me on the back.

"Fantastic, Manny! Wait till you see what happens now. I had a real professional shoot your magic move. Whoa, my man! Different venue, different outfit. YouTube's gonna explode all over again!"

Can't believe this. Didn't think this thing could get any bigger, but now what? Where is this heading? Always dreamed of being a rock star. With Waldo and the magic move, I think we're getting close.

I celebrate with Billy and Crash. We knock back a few beers. Crash, as usual, disappears. Billy and I decide to go back to the hotel, shower, and party in my old college town. Man, if the professors at Berklee could see me now!

We hit the stage door exit and emerge into the summer night. But we don't get far. Two drop dead gorgeous young girls jump in front of us. I recognize them immediately. I mean, I don't *know* them, but I can't forget how they were *cavorting* in the front row, center stage.

"Hi, Manny! We *love* you!" They look at Billy. "And you're the bass player. You guys are huge!"

Billy laughs. "Well, I'm huge. Manny's just kinda tall."

The girls giggle. "Where are you guys going tonight?"

I sigh. "Goin' back to the hotel, then we got plans."

Suddenly I'm almost lifted off the ground by Billy. He pulls me aside. "Manny—*they're* our plans!"

"Hey, man, I got a girlfriend."

Billy whacks me on the shoulder. "Well, if you remember, this big whale doesn't. Come on, Manny, you gotta help me. Let's let 'em walk back to the hotel with us, and then you can do what you want."

I sigh. "Alright. Whatever."

Guess this is what the life of a rock star looks like. Seems like Billy could get used to this.

Ten minutes later, me and Billy and the two babes kick back in the hotel lobby bar. The girls' names are Aimee and Jeri. They're both 21 and going into their senior year at Boston U. We listen to them gush about how we're going to be the biggest band since the Beatles, and that I'm gonna be the next Elvis.

Billy orders Long Island Iced Teas for everybody.

Jeri says, "I don't want tea, Billy. I want a drink."

Billy laughs. "Don't worry. This has got five different liquors in it."

Aimee and Jeri smile. For the next 10 minutes, they talk about their classes, their favorite bands, the weather in Boston. I'm half listening, but mostly I'm thinking about business. I know our performance tonight is gonna help.

Billy starts to order another round, but I excuse myself.

"I'm calling it a night." Aimee looks severely disappointed as I head for the elevators.

Twenty minutes later, as I'm just getting out of the shower, I hear a knock at the door. I throw on the cushy, terrycloth, complimentary hotel bathrobe. Gotta be Waldo, probably with an update on "magic move mania."

When I open the door, I see Aimee. "Aimee! How did you know this was my room?"

"Billy sent me up."

"And, uh, Billy and Jeri are—"

"They're in Billy's room. Jeri is my ride, so I thought I'd come and spend some time with you."

Well, I'm staring at her tight T-shirt and her shapely tanned legs, and before I can respond, she's slipped into the room. I'm suddenly aware that all I'm wearing is a bathrobe.

"Um, uh, why don't you just sit in the chair while I go get dressed?"

I grab some clothes out of my suitcase and head to the bathroom. As I'm getting dressed, I'm thinkin', I'm gonna have to learn how to handle these groupies. It's just gonna get worse from here.

So I exit the bathroom and I'm shocked. Aimee is lying on the bed, stripped down to her bra and panties.

"What the hell are you doing?"

She frowns and then smiles. She slides off the bed and seductively strolls over to me.

Whoa. I can't believe what's going on. An hour and half ago, I was on stage, watching this girl dance in the front row. Half an hour ago, I was downstairs having a drink. Now I'm two feet away from this almost naked woman, and—

I exhale and turn away from her. I just want to get out of here, but this is *my* room. "Aimee, I can't—"

She tilts her head, and smiles. "What's the matter, Mr. Rock Star?"

What's the matter? Well, for starters, I've got a girlfriend. And secondly, there's an almost naked woman in my room. I've got to deal with this. Now.

"Aimee, you've got to get dressed, and get out of here."

She takes a step closer to me. "What's the hurry? The concert's over. And Manny, you were *so* great. Gosh, you rocked." And she starts playing the air guitar, right there in her bra and panties.

I can't believe what I'm seeing. I can't help but think that *if* this was before I met Sheila, I'd be loving this. An air guitarist with curves. And man, does she have curves. Wow. Maybe I should enjoy the show for a while. This isn't gonna go any further, right? I look at her and shake my head, and I go and sit in the corner chair.

Aimee puts down the air guitar and saunters to the bed. Uh-oh. I hope she doesn't lie down. Fortunately, she sits. She starts talking in a soft voice, but I'm not hearing a word she's saying.

It would be *very* easy to sleep with her, but that would be a terrible thing to do to Sheila. Sheila's the best thing that ever happened to me. This would kill her. This would kill our relationship. But only if she found out. And she never would. She's a thousand miles away. But—

Aimee gets up, comes over, and takes my hand. She tries to pull me up, but I don't let her. But now I'm afraid she's gonna fall on top of me. I sure don't want that, so I get up from the chair, and we're face to face.

"Manny, you're so good looking. You're a star, and soon you're gonna be a *big* star."

There are a million reasons not to do this—I don't even know this girl, I'd be cheating on Sheila, this chick could get pregnant. Ah, that's it.

I look at Aimee. I struggle to keep my eyes above her neck. "Listen, I don't want to get you pregnant."

She puts her hand on my shoulder, and lets out a low laugh. "If that's what you're worried about, that's not a problem." She smiles. "I'm on birth control, silly."

"Um, uh—"

She starts running her fingers through my hair. I put my arms around her. Her skin is warm and smooth. I haven't had sex since I started dating Sheila, and that was four months ago. I can hardly think straight.

Her lips move forward. Should I resist? She persists, and I figure, what's the harm in a kiss?

Half an hour later, Aimee got what she wanted.

24

♩·♪ *Yesterday is gone and*
tomorrow may never be
So today I ask what do you want from me?
What's this heart to do? ♪ 𝅝·

"Live to Give"
— Michael James Mette (Bring Forth the Light)

I wake up the next morning, and I'm wonderin' what the hell I'm going to do. Aimee's still asleep, but it's not Aimee that I'm thinking about. I'm never gonna see her again. I'm thinking about Sheila. I'm *definitely* gonna see her. Am I gonna tell her? Would she ever want to see me again? Will this be the end?

I decide to shower and dress before I wake Aimee. When I come out of the bathroom, she's already up.

"Aimee, what are you doing with my phone?"

"Just putting your number in mine. Nice phone."

I'm ticked. "Aimee, you got to get out of here! I got to pack. Our flight leaves in less than two hours."

Aimee is clearly disappointed. "Are you sure you don't have *any* time?"

"Listen, Aimee, I really gotta go."

Fortunately, she doesn't argue. "Okay, then, I've gotta meet Jeri anyway." She walks out. Good. Finally.

Fifteen minutes later, Billy is at the door. "Wow, what a night, Manny. Did you have fun with Aimee?"

"Billy!" I yell. "Why did you send her up here?"

Billy frowns. "Well, I had to get rid of her if I wanted Jeri to come to my room."

I'm pissed. "Don't you *ever* give anyone my room number."

"Manny, why are you so upset? Didn't you have fun?"

"Billy, you know I'm with Sheila."

"Yeah. Well, uh—you didn't have to sleep with the girl."

I almost explode. He's damn right—and that *kills* me. But if Billy hadn't sent her up to my room—. "Listen! I don't want to talk about this anymore. I'll see you in the lobby."

———— ♪ o 𝄞 ————

Sitting on the plane waiting for takeoff, I see the second wave of the "magic move" explosion on the internet. Wally 'Waldo' Wallace was dead on. The quality of the video is spectacular. Between Waldo's publicity and the tweets of Steve and his followers, the video is seen by millions overnight. I should be ecstatic. But deep down, I'm wracked by guilt. And before takeoff, I'm talking to the only woman I've ever loved.

"Why didn't you call me last night? I was dying to know how it went."

"Sheila, it went great. I'm sorry. Afterwards, uh, Billy and Crash wanted to celebrate, and, you know, it got kinda late, and, uh—"

"Oh, it's okay." This makes me feel worse. She could be jumping down my throat for not calling, but instead, it's 'okay.' "Manny, I saw the new video! It's fantastic!"

"...Ladies and gentlemen, at this time, please turn off all electronic devices..."

"Sheila, we're about to take off. I've got to turn off—"

"I know. I heard. Love you."

"Love you, too." I feel sicker than ever.

Well, there I am, strapped into my seat with nothing to do but think about what I've done. I mean, I've had sex with quite a few women, but it was always pretty much understood that there would never be any future to it. And I was always fine with that. After I lost my mother at 14, I never believed that any relationship with any woman would ever last forever.

But my time with Sheila changed all that. She really is the first woman I've ever loved. And when you love somebody, the last thing you want to do is hurt them.

Sheila's incredible. It can't be easy for her to resist doing it with me. And yet, some chick I don't even know strips down and kisses me, and I totally cave.

Why did I sleep with that girl? I'm so weak. One night away from Sheila and I'm in bed with someone else. The way the band is going, I'm going to be on the road *a lot*. If I cave on the first night, what am I going to do the rest of my life?

161

And what am I gonna do now? If I tell Sheila, she's *really* gonna be hurt. It *kills* me to think about that.

So, what if I don't tell her? There's no way she could find out. But can I live with myself? I don't think I can.

But if I tell her, she's gonna leave. Can I live *without* her?

By the time we land, the decision is made.

CHAPTER

25

~ *Sheila* ~

It's hard to concentrate at SVDP after seeing a voicemail from Manny pop up on my phone. He must have landed! A flutter rushes over me when I think about seeing him. I listen to his message.

"Sheila, I've got to see you. It's important. Meet me at Lafayette Park, on the bridge, right after work. No need to call back unless you can't make it."

Wow, that was weird. I hope he's okay. I'm gonna make a quick visit to the chapel before my lunch break. I move to the front and kneel in the Presence of Jesus and feel a sense of relief just being here.

"Lord, I don't know what to think of this message. You're blessing Manny with *incredible* success. Things are happening so fast. I can't wait to see him. But he said it's important. What could it be?

"Lord, he's exploding again on YouTube. Is his new agent going to want him to move to California? Wow. Would he leave me to move? Would he ask me to go with him? If he did, would I go? Would I just *drop everything* and go? And what if I didn't? Would he leave me then? Would he find someone else?

"He said to meet him on the bridge. Lord, that's where we had our first date! Is he going to ask me to marry him? What if he did? Is that Your Will for me, Lord? Do I say yes? He's going to want an answer.

"Lord, I'm just not sure what this is all about, but I am *so* glad that You are with me. You are my True Love. As always, I need Your grace.

"Right now, just help me to make it to five o'clock. And Lord—please help Manny to do whatever he needs to do."

26

*White clouds, dark clouds,
    clouds of menacing gray,
I'm looking for the sun,
    am I gonna see it today?
Will anyone see it today?*

"Clouds"
— The Dukes (Manny Morrison)

I'm standing on the little bridge over the pond at Lafayette Park, wishing with all my heart that Sheila and I could enjoy the wonder of the ducks swimming below, and look at the flowers, and wander among the trees, and bask in our love. But that's not possible. And it's all on me.

On any other day, Sheila would be strolling toward me with a smile that lights up the park. But today, she has an uncertain look on her gorgeous face. She takes my hands as we meet. Oh, if things were only different.

She immediately makes it clear she wants to know what's going on. "Hi. So you told me we needed to talk—in person." She gives me a quick smile. "Well, here we are."

How do you tell the person you love that you cheated on her? I've been thinking about how to do it for hours, but there's no easy way.

"Sheila, I love you. And, uh, because I love you, I always want to be honest with you. I always want to tell you the truth." I can tell by the look on her face that she just wants to know what I have to tell her.

"Sheila, I couldn't live with myself if I didn't tell you the truth, so here it is." I swallow hard. "After the show in Boston, um, Billy and I went back to the hotel, and there were these girls, and, uh, they followed us, and, um—" my eyes fill with tears "—I slept with one of them."

I feel her hands drop out of mine. It's hard for me to look at her. I start babbling. "I didn't want to, really, you see, Billy was with this girl, and her friend came up to my room. Her friend had their car keys, and she, well, she—"

"Manny, I don't want to hear it. I've heard enough." She groans in anguish. She pounds her fists against my chest. Then she shouts in anger. "Manny, how could you? How could you do that to me?"

I have no answer. I see the hurt—and the anger—in her eyes. Can't bear this. I look at my feet.

"Manny, I've been saving myself for you. You may not understand this, but I've been saving myself for you *my entire life*. And *you* just go off and *sleep* with somebody?! I thought you loved me."

"I do—"

"Well, people who love each other don't run off and do this!"

166

"Right. I know. Of course, you're right. And, um, I will never do this again—"

"Not with me, you won't. Manny, I thought we were going to make it. But I can't be with a man who's going to go on the road, and I'm not going to know what the hell he's doing, and I have to think about what he's done to me before, and—"

She throws up her hands and walks away.

I'm still standing on the bridge, but the love of my life is gone.

27

~ *Sheila* ~

"I *cannot* believe he did this! This is unbelievable. How could he possibly—?" I scream into the cold lonely air of my apartment before I drop to my knees and just sob.

"I *trusted* him. Ooooh! I *never* thought he'd—. How could he *do* that? *Why* would he do that? What a *jerk!*"

I start beating the floor with my fists. "How could he *possibly* do this to me? Why the *hell* did I trust him? The *first* concert I'm not with him, and he goes to bed with some *groupie!* Ooooh! He's not the man I thought he was. He's *nowhere near* the man I thought he was! How could I *possibly* trust somebody who would do *this*?"

I get up only long enough to collapse onto my living room couch.

"I can't believe I was *in love* with this guy. I actually thought for a moment he was going to ask me to *marry* him today. Ha! Boy was I wrong. How could I fall in love with someone who—who would do this? I was *sure* he loved me. I was a *fool!*"

After my initial burst, I feel the need to talk to someone. I pick up the phone to call Rachel, but then let the receiver fall out of my hands. I'm too weak to explain it all to her right now. Instead I have it out with God.

"Lord, I'm *devastated.* Do you hear me? *Devastated!* I don't know where to go from here. It's going to take me a *long time* to get over this. And to get over *him.* Why did this have to happen? He was so right in so many ways. It hurts *so much* that he betrayed me. And Lord, it hurts *so much* that it's over."

28

 Life and love were in the air,
Before it all came crashing down.

"The Fall"
— Manny Morrison (age 20)

It's so hard to live without Sheila. Two weeks later, me and Billy and Crash fly to California to record at Jupiter Records, and on the plane, my deepest thoughts are about how tremendous it would be to share this with her. How I'd love to have her with me. How crushing it is not to be able to talk to her.

But throughout my life, whether things are good or bad or terrible—and without Sheila, they're *absolutely* terrible—I always have music to fall back on. We have a job to do on the coast, and we get it done.

The sessions are long and intense. If you've never recorded in a studio, you have no idea how exhausting the work is. Putting in 10- and 12-hour days, we knock out our 12 songs in seven weeks. Next, they tell us the producers will spend about six or eight weeks mixing and re-mixing and mastering it all, so we have no exact release date.

Anyway, we don't have a lot of time to enjoy the sandy beaches of the Pacific, but we do make it out a couple of days. Boy, are we a sight. Billy looking like Porky Pig, Crash looking like a 140-pound wraith, and me—looking like a rock star, although I hardly feel like one. Oh, sure, the bikinis catch my eye, but each time I think about having sex, I remember why Sheila isn't here with me.

In the dark days without Sheila, Mr. Six proves to be my best friend. While I'm recording and Steve is into the new season, we text pretty much every day. I'm thrilled—but not all that surprised—that Steve once again *rocks* the pro football world. He catches six touchdown passes in his first three games with St. Louis, and the Rams are undefeated.

When we get back to St. Louis, Steve is there for me. He tells me that I've *got* to get my mind off Sheila. He says he's gonna help me. He's renting out a ballroom at the Renaissance Hotel and throwing a huge party Monday night. I'm reluctant to go, but he all but forces me. "Manny, this is just what you need. The crowd's gonna be hot. I'll pick you up at 8:30, and we'll make our grand entrance."

Monday comes, and I can't think of an excuse not to go, so we drive downtown. Steve flips the valet $50 to take care of the Lamborghini. Good move. The Renaissance Hotel is a very nice place, but there are abandoned warehouses not too far away, and punks and thugs on Washington Avenue may be looking for trouble. Or, just Lamborghini hubcaps.

Anyway, we walk in and I can't believe the scene. The general attire is upscale, flashy, and revealing. Servers in tuxedos wander around with trays of exotic hors d'oeuvres. There's a bar in each corner of the room. It seems like every person is already holding a drink.

The crowd looks like a St. Louis celebrities' Who's Who. 15 or 20 of Steve's teammates, all of them basking in the glow of the Rams' winning streak, pepper the room. Half-a-dozen NHL stars are here, too. Apparently the St. Louis Blues' best players are now among the friends and fans of Steve Bronson. I see the mayor, surrounded by staff. He's smiling as if he'd like to see more events like this. There are local actors, TV news anchors, radio DJs—whoa.

And then there are the women.

Some of them are probably Rams cheerleaders. Each hairdo and makeup job probably took hours. They look like they're competing with each other to see who can show the most cleavage, wear the tightest top, or prance in the shortest skirt. And many, no doubt, have seen *me* on YouTube.

When I was younger, this is what I always wanted. The fame. The parties. The girls. Everyone having fun. And the way our music is going, this could be me every weekend. But right here, right now, it doesn't feel like those parties that I dreamed of.

Everyone's drunk. The guys are just looking for the hottest girl, and the women are looking for famous faces with fat wallets. All anyone is thinking about is who they're going to go home with.

So, as Steve gets mobbed, I quickly slip off into the men's room. I sit down in a stall without even dropping my pants. Need time to think.

It's an amazing scene out there. But I'm the loneliest guy in the place. Not into it at all. Now, you may think it's good that I've matured past the point of desiring only sex, but that doesn't even enter my mind. I'm suffering—wallowing—in the misery of having blown it with Sheila, and having to live without her.

I slide out of the men's room and into the kitchen. Some of the waiters recognize me. I tell them I'm not feeling great, that I need a strong drink. Don't know what they give me, but I toss it down. Then they oblige me with another one that seems even stronger, and I make that one disappear.

I peek back out to the party and I know I can't bear to walk through that crowd. Gotta get out of here. I know that even on a Monday, there will be people walking the side-walks of Washington Ave, but I don't want to see *anybody*. I ask a waiter if there's any way I can slip out the back.

He leads me through the kitchen to a short stairway which leads to a door that exits into a long alley. Great! Not a soul around. It's perfect. I thank the guy, and I start out on a slow walk. My head is a little buzzed, my eyes are down, but I'm alone. Which, if I can't be with Sheila, is exactly where I want to be.

Is this how people feel before they commit suicide? I have no idea. I try to shake myself. I'm not goin' there.

Well, I could, but—no. Unh uh. I'm a long way from doing that. I think.

Damn those groupies. I need *friends*. At least I got Steve. Yeah, he's into living the wild life, but I know he's a friend, and he cares. And I've got the band. We're on Jupiter Records—how many people can say that? So—I guess I've got *something* to live for. I guess.

"Manny."

A male voice cuts through the silence from behind me. But I'm not gonna turn around.

"Manny!"

Whoever it is, he sounds like he's only about 10 feet away. The voice is now a bit louder, and has a touch of urgency. Shit! Who *is* it? Sounds like a voice I vaguely recognize—.

"Manny, you can stop walking."

I don't like his tone. I stop and turn around.

"Jenkins!" I exhale. "Wow, Sonny, you scared me. What are you doin' here?"

He's got this hollow grin on his face. "The question is, what are *you* doin' here, Manny? I figured I might find you at the party, but a dark alley? You're making it too easy for me."

I feel sweat beginning to form on my forehead. "Uh—too easy? What do you mean?"

He slides his hand inside that same old damn plaid jacket and pulls out a gun.

In an instant, I know how people have heart attacks. My ticker is pounding like it's about to crash through my chest. Suddenly, it's hard to breathe. I swallow hard.

"Sonny! What are you doing? What are you doing with a—"

"You fired me, kid. Remember?" Jenkins is snarling. In the moonlight of the alley, he barely looks human.

"Sonny, I uh, no. I just, uh, I just got somebody else to—"

He cuts me off with a growl. "Yeah, to represent you. After I got you to the brink of the big-time—you dumped me."

Gotta respond. What can I say? No time to think. But if I say the wrong thing—. "It was, um, a business decision, Sonny. Nothing personal."

He grits his teeth. "Right. Well, let me tell you somethin' about *my* business. I find young, dumb suckers like you who can strum a guitar and make noise on stage. When they get good, I turn 'em over to my boss, and he *handles* their contracts, if you know what I mean. But you got smart, Manny. Too smart. You went with someone else."

I can't believe this. "Um, Sonny, I wasn't looking for anyone else, um, this guy came to me—really!"

"Yeah, and when he did, you threw Sonny under the bus. Punks like you think you can get away with shit like that. Manny, you were gonna make it. You would have made millions. You were good. But now—never gonna happen. And all because you screwed Sonny." He's shaking his head. "Oh, what a shame."

I'm in a panic. What can I do? My mind is racing. "Sonny, don't—let's talk."

175

"No time to talk, Manny. You talked when you fired me." He takes one step forward and points the revolver toward my chest.

I frantically consider the options. I can suddenly move to tackle him. But I'm not quicker than a bullet. And he's not gonna miss from 10 feet. Gotta use words.

"Sonny, please! Please! Put the gun away, and let's go talk. We can—"

"The time for talking is over. I may no longer manage Manny Morrison, but this way, *nobody's* gonna manage you.*"

He cocks the gun. The soft click reverberates through my skull. I'm aware that it's going to be the next-to-last sound I hear on earth. The gleam of the moonlight off the gun barrel hits my eyes. I take in every bead of sweat on Jenkins' forehead. He clenches his teeth. His eyes narrow into small black slits.

A million thoughts start whipping through my mind. I raise my hands up into a position of surrender. I start to shake. I feel paralyzed. I know the shot is coming. Memories from my life pour through my consciousness. I'm playing my toy guitar as a little kid. Watching my mom die. My dad's funeral. Singing in dive bars. Playing the big arenas with Billy and Crash. My first glimpse of Sheila at Kaldi's. Praying with her in those churches. Her face when I crushed her with my confession. No! It can't end like this.

Jenkins lifts the point of the gun slightly, and then starts to bring it down to shoot. I hear the gunshot—but it misses me! By a lot!

176

A nanosecond before he pulled the trigger, a blur roars in from behind Jenkins and knocks him to the concrete. The gun goes flying. I see a huge man on top of him, pinning him to the ground. I can't believe it! Tears of joy and relief consume me.

I have never been happier to see a pair of overalls in my life!

I see Jenkins attempt to get up, but he barely moves Oscar's 270 pounds.

"Whoa, there, boy!" Oscar says with a grin as he pins Jenkins' smaller frame against the cement. "Don't make me get out my can of Whoop-Ass!"

29

♩ ♪ *You know my soul, you see my shame,*
   but still you love, you love me just
   the same. ♪ 𝅝·

"Changed by You"
— Michael James Mette (Bring Forth the Light)

So, I'm at the police station until four o'clock in the morning. After the cops heard the shot in the alley, and picked Jenkins out from under Oscar, they bring me and Jenkins in. They believe me when I tell them he tried to murder me. They book Jenkins and put him behind bars. I trust Jenkins will have a good time in jail until the case goes to court.

Now, I'm no Detective Columbo, but, since the gun was fired and Jenkins owns the gun, and the only fingerprints on the gun are Jenkins', and Jenkins has a motive, well, not even Perry Mason is gonna get Jenkins off.

The biggest problem at the police station is trying to explain how Oscar just disappeared. I try to tell them that he does that all the time. After a while, they just shrug and let me go.

Well, when I get home, I'm shaken up and exhausted. I silence my phone, throw it on the nightstand, and hit my bed.

I wake up shortly after noon and check the phone. I have a couple of missed calls from a number I don't recognize. Then I see these texts, one from Billy and one from Crash.

"Hey man, sorry to hear about Steve, hope he's okay."

"So sad to hear about Steve. I never pray, but I'm gonna pray now."

What the hell? I go to the website of a local TV station. The top headline reads: "Rams Superstar Critical after Crash."

I click on the news video. The TV reporter is standing outside a hospital. "Rams' wide receiver Steve Bronson, affectionately known to his fans as 'Mr. Six,' is in intensive care here at Barnes Jewish Hospital after a one-car crash last night. Police say Bronson's Lamborghini skidded off Highway 40 and slammed into a tree at a high speed." They show pictures of Steve's car, totally demolished. I almost throw up. "Bronson was driving alone. Hospital officials here say Bronson is listed in critical condition in the ICU. They are not releasing any other details about his injuries."

Hang in there, Steve. Hang in there, pal!

I'm at the hospital in record time. Chaos reigns outside the entrance. Looks like every TV satellite truck in town is here. Reporters are holding mics, getting ready for more live reports. There's a barricade holding back

179

dozens of fans who are, what? Praying? Hoping? What? Police and security guards are everywhere.

Gotta see Steve. Gotta get to him.

I'm stopped at the entrance. Burly security guard. "Hey, where you goin'?"

"I gotta see Steve Bronson. I gotta—"

"What's your name, pal?"

My name? "Manny Morrison. I've—"

The guard holds up his hand. "Manny Morrison? Let me see some ID."

"ID? Why the hell do you—"

"Just shut up, and show me some ID."

This is weird. I whip out my wallet and show him my license.

"Okay," he says, suddenly putting his arm around my back. "Manny Morrison and family are the only people I'm supposed to let in. Steve's request. Come with me."

The ICU is on the fourth floor. Mr. Security is proud of himself. "I got Manny Morrison here."

A nurse escorts me into a specialized ICU unit. And I gasp.

I know the man I am looking at is, indeed, Steve Bronson, but he barely resembles his superstar self. He wears a white bandage wrapped around his forehead, covering up much of his blond locks. His eyes are closed. His face is marked with about 20 cuts and scratches, most of them small, with the notable exception of a gash that runs from his right temple down to his chin.

His right arm is in a cast, bent at the elbow and resting

across his midsection. His left leg is elevated a couple of feet above the mattress. It's wrapped completely in some kind of white substance—is it heavy bandages or some kind of plaster?

"Mr. Bronson, you have a visitor," the nurse says in a soft voice.

Steve lets out a low groan, then slowly manages to open his eyes.

His level of alertness increases dramatically when he recognizes me. I'm stunned to think that I mean so much to him.

"Manny! Oh, Manny. Thanks so much for coming." He grimaces in pain.

"Take it easy there, bro. Wow, looks like you ran into something that didn't move."

Steve gives me a slight grin. "Yeah."

The nurse excuses herself after issuing a caution. "I can't let you stay too long. He needs his rest."

Steve doesn't bullshit me. "Drank way too much at the party. Drove too fast on the way home. Went over the embankment and plowed into a tree. I'm lucky to still be here, man."

I'm thinkin' that makes two of us.

"Steve, the whole world knows you're here. The hospital is withholding all info, other than to say you're critical. You're, um, you're gonna make it, right?"

"Well, I've already come back to life. They told me I was clinically dead for three minutes. That's a long time."

"Whoa!" I'm stunned beyond words.

"Yeah. Amazing. But I'm back. Now, the biggest concern is my leg. It's bad. They've saved it for now, but they say if infection sets in, they may have to amputate." I see tears form in his eyes.

My eyes immediately well up. I'm stunned. No leg, no career. No leg, well, I can't imagine how tough it would be for such a gifted athlete, such an amazing All-Pro, to go through life—

"But Manny, something more important happened last night—and that's why I wanted you here."

Huh? What could be more important than being dead for three minutes? And being in danger of losing a leg?

"Listen, pull up a chair, and pull it up close."

Steve straightens up a bit in the bed. Quite a bit of color returns to his scraped-up face. His eyes seem clearer now. I have no idea what he's about to tell me, but I sense it's something important.

"Manny, I don't know how to tell you this, and I know it's gonna sound weird, but while I was in a coma or dead or something last night, I had this—this—wild 'dream.' I don't want to call it a dream, because it was much stronger than a dream. It was far more vivid and, well, different than any dream I've ever had—and in my life, I've had some wild dreams."

"I can only imagine. Well, okay—what was it about?" Can't wait to hear this.

"Well, in this vision, or whatever it is—I'm being ushered down a long, narrow, white hallway by a guy in a white suit. I'm feeling kind of excited, like, something big is about to happen. Well, at the end of the hallway, the guy opens a door, and we walk onto this dazzling set of the TV show, 'Jeopardy.'"

I wonder what meds they've got him on. "Huh, Jeopardy!" I chuckle.

"Now, don't laugh, because this was clear as a bell—and it's clear as a bell *right now*."

I don't know what to say.

"Listen to me, Manny. Please, listen to this! In this vision, I'm going to be a contestant on 'Jeopardy.' This is all crystal clear. I move to the contestants' panel, and they put me in the middle position. I ask if they're going to put "Mr. Six" on the name identifier, but they say no, it'll just be "Steve." Okay, no problem. Well, the other two contestants are suddenly standing in place. On my left is this beautiful lady, dressed in blue, wearing a rosary around her neck. She says her name is Mary. And on my right is a man who looks like he's in his early 30s, brown hair, brown beard. I didn't catch his name.

"So I look to the podium, and I expect to see Alex Trebek. But no, in his place is this older guy with white hair and a close-cropped white beard. Handsome as a movie star, but he's no one I recognize. He's wearing a classy, crème-colored jacket over an expensive-looking lime green shirt."

Steve stops talking. Looks like he's deep in thought. "Pretty cool dream, Steve," I say, mildly amused.

"Seriously, man. Stay with me, there's a lot more to it than that. So the guy standing in for Alex Trebek, I guess you'd call him the moderator, says, 'Let's play Jeopardy!' and I'm thinkin', 'Alright!' Well, the 'answer board' lights up in front of us. Looks just like it does on TV, except it's bigger and brighter than I imagined. Must be in super high-def or something.

"Well, the 'answers' begin coming up, and I'm on an *incredible* roll. I hit the buzzer on every answer, and in classic 'Jeopardy' style, I instantly provide the correct, corresponding question."

"Wow," I say. "Did you make the All-Academic team when you were at USC?"

I watch him roll his eyes. "Are you kiddin' me? I majored in football and minored in women. I had brains, but I didn't bother to use them." He sighs. "Anyway, on this edition of 'Jeopardy,'" he smiles, "it's like I'm *infused* with knowledge. I didn't even have to think hard, yet I knew *all* the answers."

"Wow. Pretty wild, Steve. I bet the other contestants were pretty ticked off that you were getting everything."

"No—and that was another strange thing. It was like, Mary and the other contestant were *cheering me on.* They never hit their buzzers. They even clapped for me. They seemed filled with joy each time I nailed a question."

"Huh, not exactly like your opponents in the NFL."

"Right," Steve smiles, and then he leans forward a bit. He grimaces as he feels the pain. "Awwww. Gotta sit back." He slowly repositions himself.

"Now, Manny, this is where it really gets wild. The moderator says, 'There's one category left. The category is, 'Illicit Pleasures.' And I'm thinking, 'Illicit Pleasures?' Great! Bring it on! And then he says, 'This is where it gets personal.'

"Well, I'm wondering what he means by that. But it's time for the game to continue, so I dive in at the top of the category. 'Illicit Pleasures' for $200. Well, the answer pops up, and it's a number. A big number. It's 4,137,886. Even though this is in a dream, or whatever, I remember that exact number as if it's written down right here in front of us."

"What's that number again?"

"4,137,886."

"And what's that number mean?"

Steve holds up his uninjured hand. "I'm getting to that. I know the correct question instantly. I'm still on a roll, so I hit the buzzer, and the moderator says, 'Steve,' and I blurt, 'How many times have I had impure thoughts about women?' And the moderator says, 'Correct!'

"Well, I'm ruffled quite a bit, as you can imagine. But I play on. 'Illicit Pleasures' for $400.' Well, the answer pops up, and it's another number, this time, 586. And again, amazingly, I know the question. I hit the buzzer and say, 'How many times have I committed the mortal sin of masturbation?' and the moderator says, 'That's correct!'

"Well, now I'm shaken up. I didn't know masturbation was a sin, let alone a mortal sin, so I say, 'It's wrong?' Well, the moderator replies, 'No, you were correct,' referring to my response. 'No!' I say. 'I meant, is *masturbation* wrong? Is it a sin? Is it really a mortal sin?' 'Yes,' the moderator says, 'it's turning inward, it's abusing *yourself* and misusing the sex organs that were created for you to give to another in *married* love.'

"Well, I feel no inclination to argue with the moderator. I lean over to the contestant with the beard, and I whisper, 'Is this show being seen on live TV?'"

I look away from Steve, and I have to laugh.

Steve says, "Hey, stop laughing! The contestant says, 'Yes, this is being seen all over the world.' I'm horrified. I suddenly want this to end. But there are only three boxes left on the board, so I press ahead. 'Illicit Pleasures' for $600. Well, on the panel, there are two numbers: 340 and 1,462. To my horror, I instantly know the question. I try to restrain myself from hitting the buzzer, but I can't stop myself. The moderator calls on me, and I say, 'How many different women have I had intercourse with, and how many times have I committed the mortal sin of fornication?' And he says, 'Absolutely correct!' Well, I know the moderator is right—I sense that this guy is always right—even more right than Alex Trebek—and I feel nauseous. I'm thinking, I never raped anybody, I was just having fun with consenting women. But in that moment, Manny, I realize—I mean, I totally *know*—that sex outside of marriage is wrong. I don't know *why* or *how,* but I just *know.* And my nausea's getting worse.

"Then I notice the other contestants are looking at me with sadness, and then compassion, and then—well, I'd have to call it *love.* I'm feeling *really* sick, and yet, I feel their love."

I see Steve close his eyes. After a moment, he opens them and sighs. "Well, there are two more boxes on the board, and even though I feel like throwing up, I have a strong desire to complete the round. So I say, 'Illicit Pleasures' for $800. The panel opens, and there's another big number: 57,987,034. Well, instantly, I'm infused with the question. I buzz and say, 'How many babies in the United States have been legally aborted in the wombs of their mothers?' 'That's correct.' says the moderator. And right away, I do not know but I wonder, how many of the 340 women I had sex with aborted babies—my babies? Our babies. And I feel like I'm about to pass out.

"I grip the contestant stand with both hands. Mary and the other contestant each grab me under an arm for support. I am *so weak,* yet, I want to finish the round. I reluctantly say, 'Illicit Pleasures' for $1,000. Suddenly—I hear bells! I've hit the "Daily Double." Even in my sickness, I sense that this could be good. So I look for the amount of my 'winnings' and I see that I'm at $17,000. What should I do? I look to Mary. She gives me this beautiful, sweet smile and says with confidence, 'Bet it all.' I let out a deep breath and look at the other contestant. He grins, and says one word: 'Yes.' I can't believe how great they've been to me! So, trusting in them, I say, 'I'll bet it all!'

"Well, the moderator seems pleased that I'm putting it all on the line. We all look at the board as the last panel is revealed. To my relief, it's not another number. It's four words: 'Forever and ever, Amen.' Well, I *rush* to hit the

187

buzzer. I even clap my hands, and I say, 'How long is eternity?' The moderator says, 'Right!' and he claps *his* hands.

"Well, I feel the affectionate hands of Mary and the other contestant on my shoulders. I'm beginning to feel a little stronger, a little less sick. It seems like some great danger is passing, and that there's hope. And then—I hear beeping."

"Beeping?" I ask.

"Yes. It was the beeping of that machine right there," Steve says, pointing to the side of the hospital bed. "It beeps to tell the nurse that I'm just about out of pain medicine."

"Ahh, you woke up."

"Yep." Steve pauses. "And I can no longer see the 'Jeopardy' set, the moderator, or Mary and the other contestant."

I sit there and study Steve for a moment. I can see that this wild "dream" is weighing on him. I've never heard of an experience, one so dramatic, one that's remembered in such great detail. "So, Steve," I manage, "what do you make of all this?"

"I don't know. Like I said, no 'dream' has ever been so real. And I've never had a dream where I remember each and every part so exactly—and so vividly. And I've never had a dream where I'm saying the word 'sin.' Manny, I grew up without any religion. Not an atheist, but just never thought much about God. But this dream sure seems—not religious, but—"

"Uh, would you say, spiritual?"

"Yeah, something like that."

At that moment, the machine on Steve's right starts beeping and a nurse comes in.

"Got to change your IV," she says. "And I'm sorry, Mr. Morrison, but I've got to ask you to leave the patient. Doctor's orders. He's going to need plenty of rest."

"Nurse, just let him stay for five more minutes," Steve says. "I'm okay."

When the nurse leaves, Steve asks me to close the door. "Manny, I gotta think about a lot of things. Gonna have time to do that now. Gonna be here for a while."

He's silent for a good minute. Slowly, his injured face ripples with worry. He's becoming emotional. He's staring down at his damaged body. Tears appear in his eyes.

"If I lose my leg, I'll never play again. Football is what I do, it's what I am." The tears are rolling down his cheeks. "And beyond that, I want to someday be able to wrap my legs around my wife, but I won't be able to do that if I only have one. I want to be able to run around in the woods with my kids—"

He's crying openly now. He's not ashamed to cry in front of me. And for quite a while, he doesn't stop. Finally, he looks me in the eye and pleads.

"Manny, *please* ask God to let me keep my leg."

Now I can't hold back *my* tears. The nurse reappears. "I'll give you another minute."

We soon pull ourselves together, and as I depart the room, Steve says, "Manny, one more thing. Can you find me a priest or a minister or a rabbi—or someone?"

CHAPTER

30

♩♪ *When you hung upon*
the cross looking at me,
You didn't die so I would
try to be someone else,
You died so that I could be
the saint that is just me. ♪𝅗𝅥·

"The Saint That Is Just Me"
— Danielle Rose (Culture of Life)

I leave Barnes Jewish Hospital and walk across the street into Forest Park. Who can I find to send to Steve? It's not like I hang around with men of the cloth. Let's see, Lenny might know somebody. Could call him, but he's on the road so much he probably doesn't know anybody here. Sheila? Sheila would know somebody, for sure, but I *definitely* can't call her.

Wait a minute! Father Max! The classic rock fan priest. And—oh yeah!—he played football at Notre Dame! Wow. Definitely the perfect guy for Steve.

But then I'm thinkin', I met him through Sheila. He's Sheila's friend. I'm sure he's heard how we broke up—

and why. I shudder. Ugh! Still, who could be better? If I go to see Father Max, he's probably gonna look at me like I'm swine, but I gotta come through for Steve.

I go the rectory and ring the doorbell. Father Max seems surprised to see me.

"Manny! It's been a while." He smiles and gives me a warm handshake. "Come on in."

When we get to the den, I say, "Father, sorry to interrupt your afternoon."

"Oh, no, not at all." He motions for me to sit down. "What can I do for you?"

Should I say something about Sheila? No. Not what I'm here for. "Father, you probably heard about Steve Bronson, Mr. Six?"

"Oh, man, I did! Yeah. Isn't that terrible? I hope he's okay."

"Well, he is, Father. I just visited him in the hospital. But he's seriously injured."

He's probably wondering what I'm doing at the rectory.

"Me and Steve are good friends, Father. And—Steve is why I'm here."

Father Max gives me a look of concern. "Do you want me to give him the Sacrament of the Sick?"

The *Last Rites?* I hadn't even thought about that. "Well, no, I don't think Steve's gonna die or anything. But something strange happened last night after the crash. Something amazing, actually. Steve had this, uh, I guess you could call it a "spiritual experience." Steve's not a religious man, Father, and he asked me to find someone he could talk to. I couldn't think of anybody who'd be better than you."

Father Max gives me a reassuring smile. "I'd be glad to talk with him, Manny."

That's a relief. "Father, thank you *so* much. He's at Barnes Jewish. Can I meet you there tomorrow?"

"Of course."

This is great. Mission accomplished. As we get to the door, I'm goin' a little nuts in my head. Should I ask him about Sheila? Should I? I've got to.

"Hey, Father—one more thing I have to ask—how's Sheila?"

He lets out a long, deep breath and looks me in the eye. "You know you really hurt her, Manny."

"Yeah, I do." Of course I do, but it still feels like a punch in the gut to hear those words. "Father, not a day goes by that I don't regret what I did."

He puts his hand on my shoulder. "We are all sinners, Manny—"

I cut him off. "How's she doing, Father?"

He looks me in the eye. "Sheila's a terrific woman. She's strong." He pauses. "Overall, I'd say she's doing okay."

———————— ♪ o 𝄢 ————————

The next day at the hospital, I introduce Father Max to Steve, and I cleverly break the ice.

"Steve, Father played football in college as a walk-on."

Steve stares at the man wearing the collar and looks surprised. "Wow, great. A football-playing priest?"

Father Max grins. "Well, don't get too excited. I played at Notre Dame."

Steve rolls his eyes and groans. "USC's most hated rival. Manny, you brought me *this* guy?"

We're all laughing now. Father Max says, "Steve, we can talk about the rivalry when you're out of this place. I know what you've done in football, but Manny told me you had a spiritual experience?"

Steve tells Father Max all about his "dream," and then pauses. "Father, I'm not religious, but from that dream, I just somehow know that all those sexual things I was doing are wrong. Can't explain it, don't know why, but I just *know.* And I wanna find out why. But first, I need to understand this—the last 'Jeopardy' answer was, 'Forever and ever, Amen,' and I gave the right question, 'How long is eternity,' and everyone got really happy—and I felt great. But why was that? What did that mean? Until then, I felt sick."

Father Max takes a deep breath. "Steve, I appreciate you sharing your experience. Here's what I see in this. First of all, God was showing you how *He* sees all those things you did. When you did them, you didn't think they were wrong. But I can show you, through the teachings of the Church, how those sins offend the Almighty.

"And you want to know why everyone got so happy in the end?" Father Max smiles. "Because our Lord is infinitely merciful. And the 'moderator' and the other 'contestants' understood that. They knew that God can, and will, forgive you for each and every sin, no matter how horrible, and no matter how many times you commit them—if you tell God you're sorry—if you make a good confession—and ask for His forgiveness."

I can see Steve listening closely. I am, too.

"And Steve, when you do that, and when the Lord forgives you, you return into His grace, and then you'll know that He wants you to live with Him, in His love, in His glorious Kingdom."

I see this look of peace come over Steve's face. "Forever and ever, Amen."

31

♪ *Through the ups and downs,*
through all the pain and gain,
Sometimes we can't be strong alone,
we need another's love,
We just need love. ♪ 𝅝·

"When in Need"
— The Dukes (Manny Morrison)

Two weeks later, there's great news on the medical front. Steve's not going to lose his leg! The docs treated the gashes and removed the dirt and the imbedded stones and pumped him full of antibiotics, and it worked. The fractured tibia and the broken arm will keep him out for the rest of the season, but the medical guys say that with a lot of rehab, he can be back on the field for training camp next summer.

Meanwhile, Waldo informs me the mix of the CD is coming along, and aside from the absence of Sheila, things are looking pretty good. So I'm just kicking back at the house when the phone rings.

"Hi, Manny. It's Aimee."

"Aimee? From Boston?" This can't be good. I wonder why the hell she's calling.

"Yeah. Hey, listen," she says. "I've been wanting to call you, but I was too scared."

She's scared? "Um, what are you talking about, Aimee?"

"I'm pregnant."

Pregnant? Her words pierce my soul. Can't be. No, no, no. I'm trying to process. At least, it can't be *my* child.

"Whoa, whoa, whoa. Aimee, when I was with you, you told me you were on birth control."

She lets out a sigh. "Yes, Manny, and I was. But the doctor told me the pill is only 98.9 percent effective, and this time it didn't work."

Oh, shit. This can't be. It just *can't* be. Dammit. What are we going to do? I'm trying to think of something to say.

"Manny, I'm about three months along. I'm starting to show. I'm in school, I'm only 21, I don't have a job, I don't have any money, I can't *afford* a child. I don't know what to do, Manny." She pauses. "I think I'm going to have to get an abortion."

Now my heart's about to come out of my chest. I suck in a huge breath and pace around the room. "Aimee! Listen to me. You cannot abort the baby."

She barely pauses. "Why not?"

"Because—it's a baby." Suddenly my brain is flooded with visions of my mom holding my hand on the sidewalk outside the abortion clinic in California trying to talk women out of killing their babies. I can still hear her saying, 'What's inside you is a child, not a choice.'

"Aimee, you can't kill the—you can't kill *our* baby."

For a second, she says nothing. "Well, what are *we* going to do? I can't raise this baby alone. Are *you* gonna move to Boston and help me take care of it?"

Wow, what should I say? What can I say? I don't want her to abort, but I can't just pick up and move to Boston. The band's here. I've got a career here. But I also can't just let her kill our child, I know that. My head is pounding. Got to buy time to think.

"Listen, Aimee, I need a little time here. Don't do anything to the baby, okay? I've got to talk to some people. Give me 48 hours. I'll call you back on Friday. I promise."

I hang up. Shit. I pound the nearest wall with my fist. Can't believe this. *Pregnant?* I thought the pill was foolproof. I shouldn't have slept with her. She shouldn't have been in my room with almost nothing on, either, but she's just a young kid. I should have gotten her out of there. What was I *thinking?* This wasn't the plan, to be a dad. Not now. Dammit!

How are we gonna deal with this? I continue to pace. That's my child in her womb. "Oh, God! Help me."

Two days. 48 hours to save my child's life.

I go straight to the hospital to see Steve. He's due to go home tomorrow. I take a deep breath before I walk into his room.

"It's good to see the patient." I try to smile. "I bet you've had enough of this place, right?"

Steve gives me a grin. "Yeah, it'll be good to be home.

They wanted to send me to a rehab facility, but I told 'em I could afford a couple of home health care workers. Told them to send me a male nurse and the oldest rehab specialist they have, so I won't be tempted." Steve smiles. "I'm becoming a changed man. That Father Max you sent me, he's been coming here every other day, and we've been having some great chats. Impressive guy—even if he did play for Notre Dame."

I get right to the point here. "Steve, I gotta talk to you about something."

I spill everything about Aimee. I try, but I can't hide the panic in my voice. Steve responds like a champ.

"Manny, when I had the dream, I figured that some of the 340 women I had sex with had possibly—no, probably—gotten pregnant. And while I was infused with the knowledge of how many I had slept with, I did not learn how many aborted. But it kills me to think about it. I'll help you any way I can."

I tell him about my days with my mom and her volunteering outside the abortion clinic. "I was about 10 years old, and mom talked to this teenager, and she eventually decided to have her baby. Mom never looked so happy." I sigh. "What can we do, Steve? What can I say to this girl?"

"I don't really know. But you know who probably does?" He throws his hand in the air. "Father Max!"

"Hmm. Father Max. That's an idea."

Steve gives me a nod. "The guy knows his stuff, and I'm sure this wouldn't be the first time he's counseled a pregnant girl."

"You're right." I scratch my head. "You know, this is really strange."

"Strange?"

"Yeah. First, I send Father Max to *you*, and now you're sending *me* to him."

Up until a few weeks ago, the last place in the world you'd find Manny Morrison would be at the rectory of a Catholic church. Now, it's like someone has left bread crumbs for me. I knock on the door, and thankfully, Father Max is there. I can tell he's surprised to see me, but just like before, he's cordial and he invites me in.

"I want to thank you, Father, for all the visits you've made to Steve."

The priest smiles. "You're welcome, but you didn't have to come all the way over here to tell me that."

"Well, that's not the big reason I'm here. *I* need your help now, Father."

Man, this is *not* gonna be easy. I wring my hands and ask if I can sit down. He takes me into the den, and I sit across from him in a chair. I paw the ground with my foot. Before long, I'm *stomping* my foot.

"Try to relax, Manny."

I take a deep breath, then another, and I tell him everything. By the time I stop talking, I'm shaking.

Father remains calm and looks at me with compassion. Just that little gesture helps. For the first time since the phone call, I begin to settle down. "Manny, we'll talk more about Aimee and the baby in a minute. I can see you're trying to do the right thing. That's admirable. And I can tell you're sorry for what you did in Boston. That's important. I want to help you get through all of this." He looks at me with kindness. "First of all, do you want to go to confession?"

I'm surprised by the question. "Uh, Father, I haven't been to confession in, like, 10 or 12 years."

Father Max smiles warmly. "That's okay."

"But I've forgotten how."

"That's okay, too. It's not hard. I'll help you. What's important is that you are truly sorry for your sins."

I look at my shoes. "Well, I'm certainly sorry that I cheated on Sheila."

"I know you are. I'm sure you are. But—you've got to be sorry for all of your mortal sins. And that means being sorry for having sex with every girl you've slept with."

I exhale. I think for a second. "Boy, Father, I don't think I'm ready to say that."

"I appreciate your honesty, Manny. Again, that's admirable."

I release a heavy sigh. "I promise I'm gonna think about it, Father, but right now, I gotta figure out what to do about Aimee and the baby."

"Right." Father gets out of his chair and walks around the room. "You know, this may sound strange, but there's this movie that hundreds of pregnant women have watched, women who were intending to abort, and it helped them change their minds."

"Huh? What's the movie?"

"It's called 'Bella.'"

"Never heard of it."

"It won the People's Choice Award at the Toronto Film Festival. It's about a single girl who's pregnant, intending to have an abortion, and through the love of a friend, she decides to have the baby. And she's glad she did."

At this point, I'll try anything, but it's gotta be something that'll work. "Father, I don't know Aimee all that well, but she may not be interested in these religious kind of movies."

Father smiles. "Oh, it's not a 'religious' film, Manny. I don't think God is mentioned the entire time. It's in no way preachy. It's just a great, touching story of two people dealing with an unwanted pregnancy."

"Well, do you really think it could help?"

"I do."

"Well, okay. But—I don't think I should just mail her a movie and hope it helps. I should be with her to talk to her."

Father Max gives me a knowing nod. "Yes, Manny. That would certainly be best."

CHAPTER

32

♩♪ *Blessed are the poor*
in spirit who are torn apart.
Blessed are the persecuted
and the pure in heart.
Blessed are the people
hungry for another start. ♪ 𝅗𝅥·

"All the People Said Amen"
— Matt Maher (All the People Said Amen)

So I take Steve up on his offer to do anything he can to help. He graciously agrees to let Aimee stay at his home, *if* she'll agree to come to St. Louis. It takes a lot of convincing, but Aimee accepts my offer of a round-trip plane ticket and the chance to stay in one of the guest bedrooms at the mansion of Mr. Six. I don't tell Aimee this, but Father Max agrees to be there, too.

When I get to the baggage claim at the airport, I barely recognize her. Instead of a tight T-shirt, she's wearing a baggy sweatshirt. Instead of a short skirt, casual jeans. That night in Boston, her hair was curled and styled. Now it hangs in a simple ponytail. She looks younger than she did then.

In the car on the way to Steve's, she says, "So, Manny Morrison, do you know my last name?"

I'm embarrassed. I don't.

"Well, it's Turner."

"Ah. Turner. That's, uh, a nice, uh, name." Man, this is awkward. Can't take this anymore.

"Aimee, I want to tell you, I am very grateful to you for coming to St. Louis. I know this must be scary—"

"Manny, it's very scary. Being pregnant is scary. Thinking about raising a child is scary. This isn't the way I want to spend my senior year."

Wow. I hardly know what to say. "Yeah. Uh, I'm sure it isn't."

"Manny, do you know you can't drink when you're pregnant?"

"Right. Because of the baby."

"Do you know what all my friends do every weekend and sometimes during the week? Can you imagine how many different excuses I've had to make up?"

Didn't think about that. "Wow. Um, I can't imagine."

"Do you know that my due date coincides with Finals Week? In my senior year?"

I'm feeling terrible for her. "Aimee, I know this is *so* hard."

We ride most of the rest of the way to Steve's in silence. I'm sick. It's only Steve's loyal friendship and the compassionate attitude of Father Max that give me any hope.

Steve greets us at the door in a wheelchair pushed by the dutiful male nurse. Steve greets Aimee as if she's his long-lost sister. "I know I don't look like I'm about to run into the end zone, but I'm really glad you came, Aimee." Father Max introduces himself and extends his hand. Through his friendly demeanor, he quickly dispels any surprise or confusion Aimee may feel at seeing a priest.

"Are you Catholic, my dear?"

"Well, no, I don't really go to church anywhere. And my parents are Methodist."

He breaks into a big smile. "Oh, some of my best friends are Methodist! I probably know your parents. They live in Boston, right?"

Aimee giggles. "Right."

"Well, that must be them!"

Steve and I laugh. This priest is good at taking away the tension.

Steve welcomes us into the exquisite foyer. "How about a house tour?"

Aimee ooh's and ahh's her way through the place. We stop in the kitchen where Steve has hot pizzas warming in the restaurant-sized oven. After we eat, we continue the tour until we end at the home theater. "Are we gonna watch a movie?" Aimee asks.

"Yeah," I say. "Father Max thinks we should *all* watch this movie. Steve and I haven't seen it yet either."

Steve flips on the automatic popcorn maker in the back of the room, and we all settle into the leather theater seats to watch 'Bella.'

When the movie ends 90 minutes later, Aimee is in tears. And I'm crying almost as hard as she is.

After we stop crying, Aimee turns to me and says, "Manny, I don't *want* to abort this baby. But I just don't know what else to do."

I put my hand on her shoulder. "That's what we gotta figure out, Aimee."

Father Max chimes in with, "Many, many couples in this situation have found a way to support God's gift of life. There are agencies that will help you with anything you need. If the two of you really want to do it, God will give you the grace to find a way."

Aimee stays at Steve's that night. Me and Father Max drive over the next morning to talk about our options. Father Max and Steve convince Aimee that finishing school won't be impossible.

"Okay, okay, I can finish school, I can deal with the social stigmas. But what about money. Children are *expensive,* and I have nothing right now."

I tell her about my inheritance and the soon-to-be-released CD, and pledge to support the baby, fully and generously and financially.

"Do you mean that?"

I look into her eyes. "Of course, Aimee. Our child is more important than money."

Her face lights up.

33

It is You in the flesh, Lord, we adore
It is You, Lord, in the flesh we kneel before.
It is You in the flesh we receive, O Lord,
It is You in the flesh, we believe.

"In the Flesh"
— John Dolan

A lot happens in the next three months. The CD comes out. It's a huge hit. Within four weeks, it hits the Top 10 list. Waldo plans a tour for next summer. Glad it's next summer, because I've got *so much more* going on.

I talk with Aimee a couple of times a week on the phone. She's strong. I go to see her in November. I meet her parents, and to be honest, *that's awkward.* The good thing is, we don't bullshit each other. They know I'm not going to marry their daughter, but they're grateful that I encouraged her to have the baby, and they're appreciative of my pledge for financial support. While Aimee and I will never be husband and wife, we develop a friendship. After all, we *are* the parents of the child in her womb.

At Christmas, Lenny and I go to Midnight Mass at

the Cathedral Basilica. I wonder if I'll see Sheila there, but she's nowhere in sight. The place is packed. I feel a strange desire to receive Holy Communion, but I don't because I haven't gone to Confession.

Ever since Sheila left me, I've been thinking about all the stuff she was trying to teach me about sex and God. Regarding that, Steve and I meet with Father Max every week to discuss the Church's teachings, including the sexual stuff and it's a real *education.*

Steve's farther down the road than me. He talks with Father about how, since his dream, he just *knows* that all those things like masturbation and fornication and abortion are wrong but he needs to understand why.

So Father Max swings into what he calls "The Theology of the Body." He says it was developed by the late Pope John Paul II, but that this guy Christopher West does a great job of breaking it down in layman's terms. He says that Christopher West was a drummer in a rock band, so I'm interested in how *he* puts it.

So we get his books and tapes. It's too complicated to tell you all that this guy West says, but one point that sticks with me is the concept that God made our bodies wonderful and beautiful, but He wants us to share them with another person *only* in marriage. It surprises me how often I find myself thinking about this. I'm amazed that Steve, who had sex with 340 women, gets it so easily. Makes me kinda wish I could be a contestant on that "other world" edition of Jeopardy.

♪ o ♭ ——————

So it's a cold day in January as I'm walking along the grounds of the park by the Mississippi River downtown. I gaze up at the magnificent Gateway Arch. The sun is reflecting off its stainless steel. I look up to the top, some 630 feet above the ground, and I almost get dizzy. And then I think about how much higher up God must be in heaven. I stand, I stare, I think.

The cold winter wind starts to cut through me. I decide to drop in to the Old Cathedral which is only about 100 yards away. As I enter, I'm surprised to see the host displayed in the gold container on the altar. Is this a special day?

I'm happy to see there's only one other person in the church. He's kneeling in the first row on the right, so I go to the first row on the left. As I sit down, I look over and I'm shocked. The other guy in the church—is Oscar! His eyes are closed in prayer.

I bolt across the aisle. "Oscar!" As his eyes open, he calmly smiles as if he expects to see me here.

"Manny! It's great to see you," he says as he slides to the right, making room for me to sit next to him.

"Hey, man, congratulations on the CD. Love it. It's great!"

I stare at him in wonder. "Listen, forget the CD, Oscar. I never got the chance to really thank you for *saving my life.* You just disappeared. Oscar, you gotta give me your number."

"I would, but I don't have a phone."

Weird. "Oscar, are you Catholic?"

"Of course I'm Catholic. I love to come here and spend time with Jesus." He nods toward the host on the altar.

I look at the host. I can't hold back. "Oscar, Steve and I have been studying the Faith with this young priest, Father Max. But one of the hardest things for me to grasp is—is that host really Jesus?"

Oscar chuckles. "Listen, I know that humanly it seems like a joke that Jesus Christ, the Son of God, the savior of the world, would make Himself into a wafer."

"Yeah, that's what I'm talkin' about."

"Well, it helps if you read the Lord's words in John Chapter 6. He said His body is real food, and His blood is real drink, and He becomes that unleavened bread to feed us. Sounds crazy, I know, and that's why so many people walked away from him in John 6 and why so many people don't believe today."

"I get that. But why would God make himself into this little piece of bread?"

Oscar smiles. "Because He loves us so much. He died on the cross to atone for our sins, Manny. And it is in the Mass that His sacrifice for us is re-presented today. And why does He use bread? Because the Lord promised us He would feed us with Himself. He loves us so much, that it isn't enough for Him to have come and died for us, it isn't even enough for Him that He be here with us up there on the altar. Manny, God loves us so much He wants to come *into* us, to be *one* with us, even more intimately than a man is with his wife. When we eat that piece of bread, God's body becomes one with ours, His blood comes into our blood, He Himself is inside us, one with us."

"That's really deep. I actually remember my mom teaching me something like that. I can hear some of her words, and I hear yours, but why should I believe it? *How* can I believe it?"

"Well, it takes faith, Manny. And faith is a gift. You've got to pray to God to give you the gift of faith. Manny, you can pray for it right now. Just close your eyes, and say, 'Lord, You are God, and I am not.' Start there, and ask for faith—faith to believe. Then open yourself to receive the gift. It can change your life."

So I drop to my knees, but before I can begin, Oscar says, "I'll pray that God gives you faith. Look—that little piece of bread up there is either a wafer or it's the Son of God. What *you* believe makes all the difference in the world."

I mutter, "Thanks, Oscar." I close my eyes. I focus on God. I try to imagine that He's seeing me. No way to know, but maybe that's what Oscar means. Takes faith. I tell God that I *do* believe in Him, some, and I ask Him to increase my belief. Haven't thought about Him much through the years, but it sure looks like He's done a lot for me. For sure, He made me, because I didn't make myself. About all I can think to do is to tell Him that I love Him. But *do* I love Him?

I kneel in silence, trying to sense His presence. For

quite a while, I get nothing. So I pray like I've never prayed before, asking for one thing—the gift of faith.

My knees are getting sore, so I sit down. Again, I close my eyes. Soon, I feel at peace. And after a while, I feel—I don't know how to put it into words—I guess, *loved by God.*

I open my eyes, I look at the host, and I fall on my knees. I'm almost overcome with wonder. Can't explain it, but I know, beyond any doubt, that I am looking at Jesus Christ! I'm here. I see Him here. The wafer still looks like a wafer, but oh, I *know* that it's the body of my Lord. I just know. And I just want to stay with Him. Just want to be with Him. Just want to shut up and enjoy His presence.

I'm suddenly aware that Oscar is gone. Not unusual. But I don't care. I just want to bask in the joy of being with the One who made me, the One who died for me, the One who was, and is, and is to come.

It seems like everything my mom taught me, everything Sheila tried to show me, everything Father Max has been saying to me and Steve, is becoming clearer.

Wow. I sit back in silence for, I don't know how long. Half-an-hour? An hour? Whatever. Filled with peace and joy, I leave the church. I genuflect for the first time since I was 14. I can't wait to talk to Steve and Father Max. And Oscar. If only he had a phone.

——————— ♪ o ♭ ———————

Before I can call anybody, Aimee's on the phone.

"Hi. Want to know the sex of our baby?"

Wow. "Yeah, sure. Have you already found out?"

"Yep. Was at the doctor's today. It's a boy, Manny!"

My mind races in a million directions. Always wanted to have a son. Not exactly in this way, of course, but it's still pretty awesome. What are we going to name him? What does Aimee think? Will he play the guitar? Play football like Steve? That boy's gonna need a father. Somehow, some way. I'm the father. Can I be there for him? *Will* I be there for him?

"Manny?"

"A boy! Oh—that's great. Don't you think?"

"Sure, Manny. I'd be happy either way. And you know somethin'? I'm looking forward to being a mom more and more."

I'm happy to hear that. *Really* happy. "Aimee, you know I'm going to take care of you and our son."

"I know you will, Manny."

"Um, we've never discussed this, but I'd like to be there when the baby is born."

She giggles. "I've been thinking about that, too, Manny. I'll tell my dad to leave his shotgun at home. You can come."

I laugh. I'm filled with joy. It *is* my son. And nothing's gonna keep me from being there.

34

♩ ♪ *This is the first day*
of the rest of your life,
'Cause even in the dark,
you can still see the light,
It's gonna be alright,
it's gonna be alright. ♪ 𝗈·

"Hold Us Together"
— Matt Maher (Alive Again)

So I'm sitting in an oversized booth at O'Connell's Pub with Father Max, telling him that the baby he helped save is gonna be a boy.

"Well, Manny, if he becomes a football player, I want you to promise he'll go to Notre Dame. None of this USC stuff. If he went to USC, Steve would never let it die."

We laugh. Then I talk about my experience with Jesus at the Old Cathedral. Father is overjoyed. "So glad you *know* that it's the Real Presence of the Lord now. Pretty much the greatest thing we can know on this earth."

And then he shares a surprise with me. "Did you know Steve's going to become Catholic?"

"Really?"

"You bet. I went to his house today for a visit, and he said he's ready. Since I've been instructing you guys for so long, it's easy for me to get him into the RCIA mid-course. He's going to come into the Church at Easter."

"You're talking about the process, there, Padre. But do you think Steve's ready to keep the Commandments?"

"Well, that's a daily battle for all of us. But I know what you're wondering—the ones about chastity. Well, I asked him about that today. He told me that since his dream, he's been thinking about all those women he had sex with—no, not in a lustful way—but thinking about how he *used* them, all for his selfish pleasure. He knows now—as you do—that sex is reserved for the married."

I rub my chin. "Well, the Theology of the Body and Christopher West stuff has had an effect on me—and obviously on Steve. No doubt it's helped him understand his dream. Well, I've been thinking about it a lot, too. And you know who's helped me with it—in addition to you?"

"Who?"

"Sheila. I tried to get her to do it with me countless times, and we never did. And yet, Father, my relationship with her was the best relationship I've ever had. By far."

Father Max grins. "Right. Fun without sex. And much more than just *fun,* if you're with the right girl. Chastity gives true love the room to grow. Even a rock star can see that."

I chuckle. I pause for a moment. "Father, I think I'm getting close."

214

"Close to what?"

He's gonna love this. "Making that confession."

———————— ♪ o ♭ ————————

So when I go into church to make my first confession in almost a dozen years, I'm sitting across from Father Max. I am aware from his instruction that while I am talking to him, he is taking the place of Christ.

So I open with, "Gee, Father, I don't remember how to do this."

"Relax, Manny. There's nothing to it. You're here, I'm here. As long as you are truly sorry for your sins, we're good."

"The last time I went to confession, I was 14. It was the year my mom died."

"You told me that's when you chucked church. It's so good that you're back."

"Right. Uh, thanks. But I've done a lot of stuff in the last 12 years."

"Yes. And that's why you're here. Manny, the church is not so much a hotel for saints as it is a hospital for sinners. You're here to be healed, to be cleansed."

I feel good about that. "Okay. But I don't know where to start."

"Well, let's look at the Ten Commandments. The first one is, 'I am the Lord your God. Thou shalt not have false gods before me.' Have you engaged in any idol worship?"

"No, Father."

"You don't worship money, do you?"

I'm surprised by the question. Guess some people do. "No, I like money, but it's not what I'm about. I think maybe my problem has been, I've lived without God. He hasn't been *my* God."

"Good. And are you sorry about that?"

"Well, yes. That day in front of the host, I felt His presence and, how can I say it—the love and the power of God—and right then, I knew I was sorry that I've been away from Him."

"Great. The 2nd Commandment. 'Thou shalt not take the name of the Lord thy God in vain.'"

"Well, I haven't sworn nearly as much as a lot of people."

"Manny, we're not here to compare. Have you *ever* taken the name of God, or Jesus, in vain?"

"Oh, yeah. I can't even guess how many times."

"That's okay. This isn't about numbers. Are you sorry for each and every time?"

"Yes. I know I shouldn't do that."

"Number Three. 'Keep holy the Lord's day.' That means, first and foremost, going to Mass every Sunday. I sense we may have had a little problem there?"

"Yes, Father. I missed *every* Sunday for about 12 years."

"And we're going to change that, right?"

"Yep."

"Good. The 4th Commandment: 'Honor thy father and mother.'"

"Did good on that one, Father!" I'm thinkin' I'm pretty much one for four.

"Manny, you've told me how much you loved your mom and dad, and that's very pleasing to our Lord. But all of us offend our parents in some ways, even small ways. Are you sorry for those times that you have?"

I reflect for a moment. "Yeah. I remember there were times I gave them trouble. I'm sorry I ever hurt them." I notice my eyes becoming moist. "I loved them, Father."

"I'm sure that you did, Manny. That's beautiful. Number Five: 'Thou shalt not kill.'"

"Well, I never murdered anyone."

"Didn't guess that you had. But there's more to it than that. Abortion comes under this one. I'm so glad you did all you did to encourage Aimee to have your baby. But in your past, have any of the women you've had relations with, had abortions?"

"Not that I know of, Father. If I knew they were pregnant, I would have encouraged them not to abort."

"Good. Ah, the 6th Commandment! 'Thou shalt not commit adultery.'"

"Never been married, so I'm okay there."

Father Max puts out his hand like he's a cop stopping traffic. "Whoa, not so fast, Manny. Ever had relations with another man's wife?"

"No. I only did it with single girls."

"Manny, that comes under this Commandment, too. You've come to understand that sex is reserved for the married, so each time you slept with a woman, you were committing a serious sin against this Commandment."

"I know. I can't tell you how much I've been thinking about that. Father—" I pause. "I am *truly sorry* for engaging in sex outside of marriage."

"Excellent. Now, masturbation is under the 6th Commandment, as well."

"Wow, that one's pretty embarrassing, huh?"

"Sure. But it's a sin against God, Manny. It's also a sin against *yourself.* Turning inward, when God wants you to save yourself, and give yourself to another—your wife, if and when you get one."

"Got it. I've certainly masturbated. But now that I know it's wrong—"

"That makes a big difference, huh? And since, out of love for God, you don't want to do *anything* that's wrong—"

"Got it, Father."

"Okay, Number Seven: 'Thou shalt not steal.'"

"Um, I remember one time, I swiped one of my dad's guitars for a few hours. He was cussing and swearing, not knowing where it was."

"Did you give it back?"

"Of course. But I made it look like it wasn't me who took it."

"That wasn't very nice."

"I know. I'm sorry."

"Let's move along. The 8th Commandment: "Thou shalt not bear false witness against thy neighbor.'"

"Never been a witness in a court case."

Father Max laughs. "Great. But have you ever lied?"

"*Ever?* Well, of course. Hasn't everybody?"

"Manny, again, we're not here to talk about everybody. Do you realize that God wants us to be truthful people?"

"Well, yes."

"When we lie, we are sinning against the truth."

"I never feel good when I lie."

"That's your conscience letting you know that it's wrong. Are you sorry for the lies you have told?"

"Yes. I like to think of myself as an honest guy."

"Right. Then no more lying, okay?"

"Check."

"Number Nine: 'Thou shalt not covet thy neighbor's wife.'"

"I've never done anything with anybody's wife."

"Okay. But let's go deeper. This commandment forbids lusting after another man's wife, and also, lusting after any woman."

"Wow, can I change my answer then? That's a really tough one, Father."

"You're right, Manny. And just because I'm a priest, it doesn't mean that *I'm* not tempted in this way myself. God made women beautiful. And we should praise Him for that. But the problem comes when we desire intimacy with a woman who is not our spouse."

"Well, I've certainly lusted after women, Father."

"In Matthew 5:28, Jesus tells us, "Everyone who looks at a woman lustfully has already committed adultery with her in his heart.'"

"Well, I guess I've got a lot of adultery in my heart."

"Yes, Manny, but again, that's why you're here. To *purify* your heart. If you're sorry for when you've lusted, even when you didn't know it was wrong, then God will forgive you."

"Okay, Father. Guess I'm going to have to clean up the way I look at girls."

"Pray for grace, Manny. If you ask the Blessed Mother, she will dispense sufficient grace from God to help you avoid this sin. That's what I do, and it works."

I suck in a breath. "Alright. Okay, gonna have to put some effort into Number Nine."

Father Max nods. "Yeah. And most of us have to for the rest of our lives. The devil uses that one to trip up a lot of souls. Okay, the last Commandment: 'Thou shalt not covet thy neighbor's goods.'"

"Okay. Um, I never really coveted Steve's Lamborghini. I mean, I'm pretty happy with the Camaro."

Father Max laughs heartily. "Okay. Great. But in the last 12 years, have you ever coveted anything that wasn't yours? Have you ever been envious of what others have?"

"Well, let's see. I used to see musicians who weren't as good as me, and they were rich and famous, and I thought, 'that should be me instead of them.'"

"Good. Now, remember that. Manny, it's very possible that you're going to have more material things than most people ever dream of. But you've still got to keep from desiring the things of others."

"Right."

"Okay. So we've covered the Ten Commandments." Father Max adjusts his position and looks me in the eye. "Is there anything else you are sorry for?"

I exhale deeply. "Well, I'm sorry for all I did to Sheila. I'm sorry I was always trying to push her to sleep with me. I'm *terribly* sorry that I cheated on her in Boston. I can't imagine how much that must have hurt her. I'm sorry that I robbed her, and myself, of our relationship. You know we really were in love."

I get embarrassed as my eyes start to water. I'm trying to hold back my tears when Father Max says, "It's okay, Manny, let it out." I break down. I think about that horrible day, when I confessed to Sheila that I cheated on her. I've never seen someone so hurt. The tears are really flowing now, but I'm not ashamed. I *can't* hold them back.

I look up, and to my surprise, Father Max is crying, too. It takes a few minutes before either of us can speak.

"Manny, we gotta finish the Sacrament here. Are you truly sorry for all of your sins?"

I exhale deeply. "Yes, Father, I am." And I mean it.

"Beautiful. Then for your penance, say one 'Our Father.'"

I'm stunned. "Um, wait a minute. I've committed all these sins against God for the last 12 years, and my penance is *one* 'Our Father?'"

"We don't need to say a lot of prayers to receive the mercy of God, Manny. Now take in, very closely, what I'm about to do." He raises his hand to bless me, and as he does, he says, "God the Father of mercies, through the death and resurrection of His Son, has reconciled the world to Himself and sent the Holy Spirit among us for the forgiveness of sins."

He raises his hand a little higher and says, "Through the ministry of the Church, may God give you pardon and peace. And I absolve you from your sins in the name of the Father, and of the Son, and of the Holy Spirit. Amen."

He makes the sign of the cross over me and I can't hold back. The tears pour out all over again. But these aren't the tears of guilt, but tears of joy—that God has overwhelmed me with His mercy.

"You're a new man now, Manny. Our loving God has forgiven you of all your sins."

CHAPTER

35

♩·♭ *We have to see beyond the walls,*
   we have to look behind the curtain,
   What looks like a stone, might be a
   diamond, but at a glance,
   we can't be certain. ♪ 𝅜·

"Behind the Curtain"
— Lenny and the Jets (Lenny Sanders)

For the next couple of months, things are great. I'm going to Mass and receiving Holy Communion every Sunday and doing what I can to keep every one of those Commandments. Steve's so committed to the RCIA that he goes to the classes in his wheelchair for the first couple of weeks. By the way, he's doing much better now, but he's still on crutches.

Our album went platinum. You know those *good* songs I wrote? Well, some of them became *great*. The years of work paid off. All those nights at home and in coffee shops, writing and rewriting, coming up with lyrics that walked the fine line between stupid and clever, melodies that sucked at first but became something that made people dance.

Wally 'Waldo' Wallace is cookin' up all kinds of things. Media stories, photo shoots, appearances, the planned summer tour. Seems like I'm everywhere.

You know, all my life, all I wanted to be was a rock star. I knew if I made it, I'd have fame, money, women. But now that I'm on top, I realize that these things are not what's most important in life. Not by a longshot.

Anyway, just when I think I've got my life on track, I see this story online, reprinted from the Boston Globe:

Police Investigating Homicide
of BU Student

Boston Police have no suspects in the murder last night of a pregnant 21-year-old Boston University student. Medical authorities claim it's a near miracle that the baby in her womb survived. The victim was identified as Aimee Turner of Needham. The shooting occurred on Boylston Street at 11 p.m. Turner was returning to her apartment from a friend's birthday party.

Turner sustained a single gunshot wound to the head. She was rushed by ambulance to Mass General Hospital, where doctors tried in vain to save her life.

The baby was delivered by Caesarean section moments before the victim died. Police say the apparent motive in the case was theft. The victim's purse is still missing.

CHAPTER

36

♩ ♪ *Son of a rock star, son of a rock star,*
will he be like me?
Will he play the crowd and take his bow,
what will he turn out to be? ♪ 𝅝·

"Son of Rock"
— Duke Morrison (Duke Morrison)

Flying time from St. Louis to Boston is nearly three hours. I'm wishing it could be even longer. I'm in shock. I can't believe this happened. What kind of creep would shoot a pregnant girl just to rob her? Who knows how it went down? I bet she refused to give the guy her purse. He probably tried to take it. I'll bet she fought him. Aimee's got a lot of spirit. I mean, she *had* a lot of spirit. Man, this is terrible. Beyond terrible. This never should have happened.

And now the baby has arrived. The *miracle* baby. No doubt, God wanted him to live! But this sure wasn't the plan. I was planning to fly to Boston for the birth. I was confident Aimee was gonna be a good mother. It was the father part I was worried about. I would send regular checks, more than adequate checks. And I was gonna fly out there to see the little guy regularly.

Now, *our* baby has become *my* baby. The poor child has *no* mother—just a single dad. A totally surprised, inexperienced, untrained, single dad.

Wow. Lord, I'm going to need Your help. Big time.

When the plane lands, I head straight to Mass General. Aimee's parents greet me as soon as I get off the elevator. Her mom is crying. Her dad shakes my hand, then gives me a hug.

"Manny, we're glad you came."

"I'm sorry. I am so, so sorry." I don't know what else to say.

The baby is in the NICU. The good-hearted nurses are well aware of the tragedy. They're giving him oodles of tender loving care. They tell me he's healthy. No perceivable problems. After eight months in the womb, his birth weight is 5 lbs., 1 ounce. They say if all goes well, he could be released within a week.

I look through the glass at my son. His face is all scrunched up, like many newborns. He's got some hair. It's brown like his daddy's. His eyes are closed. Seems like he's enjoying his sleep.

The head nurse approaches. She puts her hand on my shoulder and says, "I've got to talk to you." Huh? She leads me into an office.

"Believe me, Mr. Morrison, we tried to keep your identity quiet, but it's gotten out. A TV station found out that you're the dad, and they're on the way over.

And that means, the others are sure to follow."

Wow. I may be a rock star—but I'm a *rookie* rock star. Wasn't even thinking about the media. What the hell do they want to know? What am I gonna say?

A professionally dressed woman walks into the room and introduces herself. She's the public relations director of the hospital. She hands me a statement she's written for me and advises me not to answer any questions. She says this is the way to do this, that it will make things a lot easier.

I look at the statement. *Who wrote this?* A bunch of lawyers?

The PR maven says, "I want to prepare you, Mr. Morrison. Soon after the first TV station called, the national news outlets jumped on this. A lot of reporters are already here. So we're moving the interview—" *Did she say interview?* "—into the media room."

She gets up to escort me. As we walk down the hall and onto and off the elevator, my head's spinning. The only things I care about are my baby and having a talk with Aimee's parents. But now they want me to address the world.

We enter the media room, and it's a circus. Fox, CNN, MSNBC, HLN and a bunch of local stations are aiming their cameras and microphones at the podium. Ms. PR maven steps up.

"On behalf of our doctors and nurses—and our board of directors—we welcome you to Mass General Hospital. We know you are all excited to talk with Mr. Morrison.

Well, he's here, and he's going to read from a prepared statement. Mr. Morrison?"

This is crazy. I walk to the podium and start to read. "Ladies and gentlemen of the media, I appreciate you being here today."

Actually, I don't. I crumple up the statement and throw it on the floor. A reporter gasps.

"I'm here today to see my son. I'd appreciate it if you would respect my privacy."

I leave the podium and walk past the PR lady and head back to see my child. The reporters are shouting.

"When's your tour starting?"

"What's the first song you're going to sing to your son?"

"Manny, are you sure you're the father?"

Welcome to the life of a rock star.

CHAPTER

37

~ *Sheila* ~

I look up to see Manny's face on the TV and sigh. No big deal. I mean, I've seen his face plastered all over TV for a while now. He's probably just being nominated for another award or something.

But this doesn't really look like an award presentation. What's going on?

"We're going to take you 'live' now, to Mass General Hospital in Boston, where the rising rock star, Manny Morrison, is about to make a statement."

What's Manny doing at a hospital in Boston?

"I'm here today to see my son. I'd appreciate it if you would respect my privacy."

I listen to a little more of the news coverage before shutting off the TV. Almost instinctively, I begin to talk out loud to God. "Lord, I can't believe this. Manny has a son? The mother was murdered? He's in Boston. It must have been that girl—. She must have gotten pregnant when—. Wow. The girl was murdered last night. Manny must have headed up there right away. This is all so hard to fathom.

"Lord, have mercy on the soul of that poor girl. And thank You for sparing that baby.

"The way Manny spoke to the media, he clearly wants to be with his son. Is he going to put him up for adoption?

"Lord, there are so many questions. Whatever Manny needs to do, *please* give him the strength to do it."

38

 You who dwell in the shelter of the Most High
who abide in the shade of the Almighty,
Say of the Lord, "My refuge and my fortress,
my God, in whom I trust.

— Psalm 91

I sit in the last row of the United Methodist Church at Aimee's funeral. The church is packed. Her parents, grandparents, their friends, neighbors. Her older brother and her two older sisters that I never met. Her childhood friends and her college friends. Never seen so many young people at a funeral. Funerals should be for old people who have lived a full life, not for a 21-year-old who had most of her life to live.

She lies in her casket up in front. I'm both glad and sad that the casket is closed. I mean, I couldn't take looking at her with a bullet wound in her head. And yet, if that bullet wasn't there, I'd like to gaze at the face of the young woman who loved our son enough to bring him into the world and raise him.

I knew Aimee for about eight months. The minister knew her for her entire life. Through his eulogy, I learn so much about the mother of my child. How she climbed a tree and saved a cat when she was eight. How she joined the church's youth group, then worked as a waitress to help send the kids on a mission trip. How her parents saved to send her to Boston U., and how she took out student loans to make up the difference.

I'm hit with the preciousness of life. How it can end in an instant. And then I think about the life of our son. How it started in a hotel room. How he came into the world as his mother was dying. Where will his life go from here?

When the service ends, I stay in the last row as everyone walks by. Aimee's body is wheeled out. Her parents walk behind the casket. Their tears will stay with me for the rest of my life.

After the burial, I tell her dad I'm going to skip the funeral reception because I don't want the college kids to make a big deal out of me. Her dad understands. He asks me to meet him and Aimee's mom later at their house. It's gonna be strange to be there without Aimee.

————— ♪ o ♭ —————

I'm still numb when I show up at their house in the afternoon. I'm not surprised that they invited me over. But I am *shocked* when I find out the reason why.

We're sitting in the living room when her dad says, "Manny, Aimee's mom and I have been doing a lot of thinking. We certainly respect that you plan to take your son home with you. But we know that you've got a very busy career. We want you to know—and we want you to know that we really mean this—that we would like to take the baby and raise him here."

I'm speechless.

"Manny, we think that you're a fine young man, and it's been great getting to know you, but—our Aimee is gone, and we know it would make her very happy that her child's loving grandpa and grandma are going to be with him every day, providing him with a wonderful life. Not that you wouldn't, Manny, but realistically, you've got a rising career to manage. I mean, look at that scene at the hospital. And you're going to be touring and cutting CDs, and, well, you're going to have a very busy life. One that's probably not suited to raise an infant."

He puts his arm around his wife. "You know, Maggie and I have raised four kids, and I don't want to brag, but I think we've done a pretty darn good job of it. We weren't expecting this, but we've talked about it, and we're ready to do it one more time."

I let out a long, low sigh. Wow. Sure didn't see this coming. I'm trying to wrap my head around this. If I just say, "Thanks, I really appreciate that," they'll take the baby, and it will be just how I thought it would be when Aimee was alive. The baby will be in Boston, he'll be well cared for, and I can visit him anytime. I can also get on with my career without the responsibilities of being a single dad.

But—that's *my* baby. It's *my* son. They're the grandparents. I'm the *father*. Sure, the easy thing to do would be to walk away—or fly away—just catch a plane to St.

Louis and get back to business. But we're talking about my son here. My *son!*

I look at Aimee's mom and dad. "I can't tell you how much I appreciate what you want to do—but I can't let you do it." I see the disappointment in their eyes. "Yes, you're a *tad* more experienced than I am when it comes to raising children, but this little guy's my son. And I want you to know—whatever it takes, I'm gonna do a *damn* good job of raising him."

39

In the center of all that I know,
I know that I know not,
There's a strong breeze blowing,
but I decide to go against the wind,
I'm a new man.

"New Man Now"
— Manny Morrison (on the plane to St. Louis)

So I'm at home sitting on the red leather wrap-around. Man, I'm gonna miss this couch. I'll be moving in five weeks. I could move to California like most rock stars, but St. Louis is a much better place to raise a kid. The new house is nowhere near as big as Steve's, but it's plenty comfortable for a man and his boy. It's a cool old place on Lindell Blvd., and on a nice day, it's walking distance to the Cathedral Basilica.

Of the hundreds, maybe thousands, of times I've sat on this couch, this is the first time I've had this kind of company—women yes, but a newborn baby, no.

I stare at the six pounds, two ounces in my hands. The doc is thrilled that he's gained a pound and an ounce in the first 10 days of his life. With no health problems. As Father Max would say, "Praise be to God."

I feel tremendous peace—and joy—as I look at my son. He's got Aimee's cute little nose and my brown eyes. His dark hair is unusually long for a newborn. Born to be a rock star? Right now he seems perfectly content to be a tiny, lovable baby. I know there'll be a little less peace when he's crying, or hungry, or wearing dirty diapers, but that's okay. I think. Right?

I'm a little overwhelmed.

Well, I guess by now I've learned from Father Max and Sheila and Lenny and Oscar and yes, Steve, that this just *might* be a good time to pray. So I say, "Jesus, my Lord, how am I ever going to be able to do this? Please help."

Grace is flowing.

I put the baby in his crib and I grab the phone to call Waldo. I tell him to cancel the summer tour. Well, Waldo goes nuts. He's yelling and screaming that I'll be passing up hundreds of thousands of dollars. I tell him I'll do maybe one concert a month and settle for tens of thousands. He tells me the world will forget who Manny Morrison is—and I tell him, I'll bet the hordes of media in that Boston hospital conference room have ways of remembering a new dad.

Besides, I think of how I would have given anything for *my* dad to be away only once a month. And I had my mom. My kid has no mother. His dad *ain't* gonna be on the road.

But I'm gonna need all the help I can get.

236

I'm grateful when good ol' Steve, a guy who understands celebrity, steps up and readily agrees to be my son's godfather. I'm sure he'll be a good one, with all the stuff they've been pumping into him in the RCIA.

As for the godmother—well, I have a pretty good idea of who *that* should be.

40

♩˙♪ *There are places you can go,*
there are places you can see,
But if you wanna know what
comforts me,
Coffee it would be. ♪ 𝅝˙

"Java"
— Manny Morrison (on the way to Kaldi's)

We haven't seen each other in nine months. We haven't even spoken. I'm thinking of spending my entire Saturday hanging around Kaldi's hoping that she will just drop in, but no—screw it—I call Sheila and ask her to meet me at our good ol' coffee shop.

She gasps when she sees the baby in my arms. I rise out of my chair to greet her.

"I'd like to give you a hug, but I kinda got my hands full here."

She responds with a smile. Her eyes widen as she gets a closer look at the baby. We sit down, and I find she's been keeping up with me.

"I found out you were a dad on the news—but I had

no idea you kept the baby."

"The grandparents offered to adopt him, but I said, 'no way.'"

She looks surprised. "Wow, Manny, that's—that's—pretty big."

She notices as the baby scrunches up his little face. He makes a tiny noise. I'm gonna call it a giggle. I give the little guy a smile.

"You pretty much look like a dad. Not bad for a rock star. By the way—I love your CD."

I'm touched. "You heard it?"

"I *bought* it. Just for the music, of course."

I laugh. "Yes, of course."

"I'm thrilled that you're doing well. And Father Max tells me you're doing *really* well."

I frown. "I thought Father Max wasn't supposed to tell anybody about confession."

"Confession? He didn't say anything about confession. He just told me you're 'a new man.' *Something* must have impressed him."

"Well, I'm not the only guy who's made some changes. Did you know that Steve is forging ahead in the RCIA?"

"Well, of course. I am a parishioner after all. But I must say, seeing Steve in the RCIA was one of the biggest surprises of my life."

"There's goodness in everybody, Sheila. You know that. It just takes some of us a little longer to figure out the right ways to express it."

She grins. I would love to know what she's thinking. It's

too much to ask. So I say, "What have you been up to?"

She says she's just been doing a lot of things with Rachel. That they were both mad that the Rams lost 10 of their last 13 games after Steve's injury. Things are going well at St. Vincent de Paul. She says she bought Terrell my CD and that he's almost worn it out. I know there must be more, but she suddenly stops talking.

After a pause she asks, "So, uh, have you gotten used to changing diapers?"

"Yep. I'm smart. Disposable all the way. Velcro, no pins. No way around that smell, though."

She laughs. "You know, Manny, your baby looks just like you."

For some reason, that almost brings me to tears. "Sheila, I've made mistakes. Boy, have I made mistakes. But Father Max helped me come back into the good graces of the Church. I really don't know how I'm gonna raise this kid, but I trust that God will help me through."

She smiles. "Manny, this is the first time I've heard you talk like that."

"Well, a *lot* has happened over the last nine months. People change, Sheila. And this baby's gonna change me a whole lot more." I look into her eyes. I swallow. I don't want to cry. I take in a deep breath, then I slowly exhale. I've got to ask her.

"Uh, you know, Sheila, this baby's going to need a godmother—and there's nobody in the world that I'd rather ask than you."

I watch as her eyes glisten. She bites her lower lip. "Manny, I didn't expect this at all."

There's a pause.

"Well, Sheila, a baby's godparents are supposed to make sure he's raised responsibly in the Faith." I give her a wink. "You *are* still Catholic, aren't you?"

She grins as a tear rolls down her cheek. For a moment, she says nothing. "Manny, if I become the baby's godmother, I'm going to have to be involved in his life, and *yours*."

"I know that."

She lets out a long, slow breath. "Manny, you really hurt me."

I wish with all my heart that I had never, ever hurt her in even the tiniest of ways, let alone—.

Suddenly, I feel her hand on my arm. "Manny—I'm going to have to think about this."

41

~ *Sheila* ~

On my way home, I call Rachel. Thirty minutes later, she's sitting at my kitchen table. As a clap of thunder rattles the windows, I share all the details of my meeting with Manny. "And to top it all off, he asked me to be the baby's godmother!"

Rachel's jaw drops. "Oh, Sheila. Wow, I don't know what to say. I think you've got to be *very* careful here."

"I know! But I really don't know what to do. And I'm sure he needs an answer."

"Of course, he needs an answer. But, Sheila, you know that if you do it, you're going to have to be in the baby's life—which means, Manny's life. Can you do that?"

That's a big question. "Rachel, if you asked me last week, I would have said, 'absolutely not.' But you didn't see him today, holding that little baby like he was the most important person in the world. You didn't hear him talk about Father Max, and how people can change."

Rachel shakes her head. "Well, seeing Steve about to come into the Church means *anything* is possible. And the fact that Manny's raising the child speaks loudly. No, Sheila, it *shouts* loudly. But still—can you be a responsible godmother, knowing that your godchild came through Manny's betrayal?"

I get a sinking feeling. "In one way, it would be the most difficult thing I'd ever have to do in my life. But at the same time, I can sense that Manny's not the man he used to be. The way he looked at that child, the way he held him, the way he looked at me—I don't know, he seems so much more *mature.*"

After a long pause, I add, "I'm going to have to pray about it. Please pray for me, Rachel. Please pray I make the right decision."

CHAPTER

42

♩⁰ *You are all that I'm not,*
  You are all that I am, Jesus!
  Break down these walls,
   take all my brokenness,
  Rebuild me to shelter Your Name. ♪ 𝄞

"Shelter Your Name"
— Danielle Rose (Defining Beauty)

In some ways, I can hardly believe that I have a son. But at the same time, I can never *forget* that I have a son. I mean, he's with me 24/7. And he's precious. I mean, *precious!* I'd barely think about using that word in a song, but it certainly fits my little guy. There are other words that fit, too, like fabulous, terrific, amazing, and—well, I could go on and on.

Whew. There are a lot of things that are kinda hard to believe right now. It's hard to believe that my son is going to be baptized here today in a place as spectacularly beautiful as the Cathedral Basilica. No doubt, this is the most beautiful place I've ever seen.

It's kinda wild that the man who's about to become my

son's godfather just happens to be the greatest wide receiver in the NFL. A couple of years ago, I couldn't envision myself even *hanging around* with anyone in the NFL.

And then there's last week's phone call—I gotta say when the phone rang, it was like, time stopped. I'll never forget it as long as I live. I waited until the last ring before I answered. I cleared my throat and said, "Hello." For a second, there was silence. Then I heard her voice—that sweet, angelic voice.

"Manny, this decision wasn't easy for me. We've been through so much, and I had such high hopes, and then—"

"I know, Sheila."

"I know you know, and that's not why I'm calling. But being a child's godmother is something that must be taken very seriously. It's a responsibility that should be undertaken only by someone who understands it, and wants to make the commitment. So, Manny, I've thought long and hard about, and I've prayed about it—"

At this point, I'm holding my breath.

"And—"

The silence seemed like it lasted forever.

"I'm going to do it. I'm going to be there for your son."

The air poured out of my lungs. It must have been the longest sigh of my life. Well, I thank her, and I thank her again, and then she cuts me off.

"Manny, there's something else I want you to know. I wouldn't be able to do this unless I could resolve, well, what happened. Manny, when you care *deeply* about someone—and I don't know if you know *how* deeply I cared about you—it's agonizing when they betray you."

My mouth dropped open. All I could do was mutter, "Sheila, I know." And I was thinking that if she wanted to describe, in graphic detail, how her heart was pierced, and how the pain went on and on, and how difficult it was for her for weeks and months—well, I was ready to hear it all.

But instead, she just goes, "There's a lot that can be said, and someday I may say it, but for now, I just want to say the most important thing—and that is, Manny, I forgive you."

The call ended seconds after that—and I lost it. I dropped my phone and fell to my knees. I started shaking. I felt the love and mercy of Sheila—and God—all at the same time. I started crying like a—well, put it this way— my little son in his greatest discomfort couldn't have out-cried me right then and there. Huh, you know, it's funny. He wasn't crying at all. He just kinda looked at me and smiled. Whew. Kids. Sometimes I think they know it all.

Well, right now, my son is giving me something else to think about. Yep, I've come to recognize that smell. I look at my watch. Got just enough time. I walk back down the side aisle of the Cathedral to the men's room and accomplish the diaper change. I'm actually getting pretty *mediocre* at this.

By the time I get back to the baptismal font, it looks like everyone has arrived. I move into position. I'm starting to get emotional here. I gaze at the guests gathered in a semi-circle.

I'm so happy to see Aimee's parents. Yes, I sent them the money for the plane tickets, but they didn't have to come. It's nice to know this baby will have devoted grandparents.

Great to see my band members here. Crash is Crash. He shows up, says nothing, but the point is, as always, he shows up. I look at Billy and my eyes get a little misty. Ever since our talk with Lenny, he's been clean. And man, there's no doubt those bass licks he laid down helped to make the CD so huge. He's still a little mushy in the middle, but who cares? He's one of the world's greatest bass players. I have high hopes that he'll meet the exact right, good-hearted woman, and they'll live happily ever after.

Then there's Terrell. When Sheila asked him to come, he probably started doing hand stands in the group home. Hope he didn't accidentally kick his staff in the head. He's all dressed up in a jacket and tie. Sure is strange to see him that way. He smiles the instant he sees me looking at him, and he starts waving like a madman. I almost crack up. The truth is, I wouldn't be where I am today if Terrell hadn't inspired me to do the splits at Burger King. Since then, 272 million people have seen me do the 'magic move' on YouTube.

There's Rachel standing next to Terrell. She looks magnificent. There's no way Rachel could *not* look magnificent. I start to tear up. She's such an incredibly loyal friend to Sheila.

I see her looking over toward Steve. She's gotta be as shocked as Sheila at Steve's sudden conversion. I'm startin' to think that *if* she'll forgive him—and give him another shot—well, you never know.

Lenny took time off from the road to be here. He's even wearing a suit. Years ago, he would have shown up in a ragged Grateful Dead T-shirt, but since he visits the Lord in churches on every road trip, he's really cleaned up his act. And I can't thank him enough for what he did for Billy.

Whenever I look at Lenny, I see a piece of my dad. Dad would be proud to be here today. Not proud about the way it all came about, but about how I stepped up and took responsibility. I'm sure Mom's looking down from heaven and smiling. She loves babies *so* much. If Aimee had aborted this child, there'd be nothing for Mom to smile about.

On the right side of the font, there he is, the godfather. Boy, it's great to see Mr. Six finally off crutches. By the way, team doctors remain hopeful that one of the fastest men on the planet will be back to revive the Rams next season.

It's hard to believe the changes in Steve. He still looks way too tan for a guy in St. Louis, but the swagger has been replaced by humility. When I met him he was all about bedding women and catching footballs, but now he takes that zeal and applies it to his spirituality. I've never had a closer friend. If he hadn't been there for me through it all—well, I don't know if I'd be standing here today. I get a tear in my eye, but I wipe it away. Don't want the big-time NFL All-Pro to think I'm a crybaby.

My heart skips a beat as I look at Sheila. She's smoothing out her magnificent, white dress. Her dark hair and blue eyes look even more beautiful than on that fateful day when we first met at Kaldi's. If I keep looking at her, I'll forget why we're here.

This baby is the product of my cheating on her, and yet here she is, the godmother. She remains the most gorgeous woman I've ever seen, and I've come to know she's so much more than that.

She looks at me with tears in her eyes, and I almost lose it. Are the tears because I'm an idiot, or because I did the right thing, or because she still loves me? There's no way I can tell. And no way to know what the future holds. I gotta look away, or this baby's gonna be baptized with my tears.

I take a deep breath. If it hadn't been for Sheila, I never would have met Father Max.

I shake my head as I look at this amazing priest! If you ask him, he'd say he's just been doing his job all this time, but the effect he's had on me and Steve has been life changing.

I slowly exhale. Okay, I'm ready. I look down at the fantastic little baby boy in my arms, and I can't contain my smile. Father Max warmly welcomes everyone, and makes the Sign of the Cross.

But before he can begin the prayers of the Sacrament, I sense someone approaching the baptismal font from behind. I turn my head to see one last figure appear. One very big man. Huh, he must save those *white, silky* overalls for special occasions.

How does he get *everywhere?* He doesn't have a phone, I don't have his address, so I couldn't invite him. I guess at this point I shouldn't be surprised to see him show up *anywhere*. Oscar winks and smiles at me as if to say, 'Where else was I gonna be today?' And again, I almost lose it.

So the time comes for me to hold my son over the font. Father Max raises a silver vessel filled with water over the baby's head.

"I ask the father, what name do you give your son?"

I say a silent prayer. *St. Vincent de Paul, pray for us.* "Vincent Duke Morrison."

Father Max smiles broadly. "Vincent Duke Morrison, I baptize thee in the name of the Father and of the Son and of the Holy Spirit."

You know, I'm not usually a touchy-feely kinda guy, but as I look at all these smiling faces, and the face of my son, I know that I have truly found love.

THE END

AFTERWORD

So, yep—it's all been kinda wild. Thanks for riding along.

In case you're wondering, my former agent, Sonny Jenkins, is in prison. With Oscar shining forth from the witness stand, Jenkins was convicted of attempted murder and sentenced to 19 years.

As for Steve, since St. Louis doesn't have an ocean or a beach, he went back to California for a couple of months to run in the sand and climb those mountains. I don't know if he ran until he puked, but he told me he's faster than he's ever been. Can't wait to see him blow by those defensive backs this season, and maybe even get the long-suffering Rams back to the Super Bowl.

Steve and Rachel? I don't know, but I'm figuring there's at least hope for a connection. Once Steve saw that God didn't want him messing around, or even *thinking about* messing around, he morphed into the kind of man Rachel would be interested in. Physical attraction is not the *most* important thing, but it is important, and they certainly have it. It'll be cool to see if everything else falls into place.

As for music, my passion is still there. When we do concerts, and Big Billy lays down that bass line, and Crash starts crushing the drums, that fire still roars within me, and I go all out to give the crowd everything I've got.

But I keep the music *biz* under control. I've just written the two best songs I've ever come up with, and we're again topping the charts, but we're only gonna do 12 shows a year, four of them in huge football stadiums. Right—very little time on the road, more time with little Vincent. I'm sure somewhere up above, my dear old dad, Duke, is nodding with approval.

We'll still make megabucks from the 12 appearances and the records. I'm gonna donate a lot of that to the effort to dig wells and provide clean water for the people of Africa.

Oh, yeah—and for the rest of his life, Father Max will never be short of funds to run the school and fix the church in whatever parishes they send him to. He certainly deserves that, and more. He helped me to clean up my soul and to realize that God loves us all, more than we'll ever know—at least in this world.

So okay, okay—I know what you're wondering. Are me and Sheila ever gonna get back together? Well, it's too soon to tell. But I do know this—she's the greatest godmother of all time. She comes over and, in that angelic voice of hers, she tells little Vincent Duke about how loving and merciful and wonderful God is. I don't think the little baby understands a dang thing that she's saying, but I figure it can't hurt. Besides, I know it helps his daddy who's listening in, and I know that's why she's really doing it. Come on, this rock star's no fool.

I know that while she has forgiven me, it's taking time for her to *fully* recover from the way I betrayed her, and to come to *totally* trust me. I'm certainly willing to give her all the time she needs. I want to show her, not only the man I've become, but that I'm *becoming* a better man all the time.

And *just* in case you're wondering—she still takes my breath away. She's the most beautiful woman I've ever known, both inside and out. And I *do* love her. So, *so* much. She's fabulous. She's *incredible.*

Through it all, I've learned that faith and hope and love are wonderful and beautiful things. And—again, *just* in case you're wondering—I'm filled with hope for her and me!

♩. ♪ God alone is my rock and salvation,
my fortress; I shall never fall. ♪ 𝅝·

— Psalm 62:3

Help us share the story of Manny and Sheila and their friends—with YOUR friends!

It's simple!
Order FREE copies of *My Rock and Salvation* at
www.matermedia.org.

If you enjoyed *My Rock and Salvation*, please ask your parents, grandparents, and others to support us with a donation so that every young adult in America can receive a copy of this novel for FREE. Donations are accepted at www.matermedia.org.

Mater Media is a not-for-profit apostolate whose mission is to create, produce, and distribute great books for FREE.